That unexpected kiss filled Melanie's head.

Adam's mouth had been hot…hungry against hers. It would have been so easy for her to allow the escalation of the kiss, but she didn't trust it. What man in his right mind would want to start something with a woman like her? She was no fool. Adam Benson was just passing time here in her house and with her. He was a cowboy boarder and nothing else. She'd gladly take his rent money, but she couldn't allow him to get into her heart in any meaningful way—because she knew with a certainty that she would never be in his heart.

Dear Reader,

As you may have noticed this month, Harlequin Romantic Suspense has a brand-new look that's a fresh take on our beautiful covers. We are delighted at this transformation and hope you enjoy it, too.

There's more! Along with new covers, the stories are longer—more action, more excitement, more romance. Follow your beloved characters on their passion-filled adventures. Be sure to look for our newly packaged and longer Harlequin Romantic Suspense stories wherever you buy books.

Check out this month's adrenaline-charged reads:

COWBOY WITH A CAUSE by Carla Cassidy

A WIDOW'S GUILTY SECRET by Marie Ferrarella

DEADLY SIGHT by Cindy Dees

GUARDING THE PRINCESS by Loreth Anne White

Happy reading!

Patience Bloom

Senior Editor

CARLA CASSIDY

*Cowboy
with a Cause*

HARLEQUIN®

entertain, enrich, inspire™

Recycling programs
for this product may
not exist in your area.

ISBN-13: 978-0-373-27805-3

COWBOY WITH A CAUSE

Books by Carla Cassidy

Harlequin Romantic Suspense

Silhouette Romantic Suspense

Other titles by this author available in ebook format.

CARLA CASSIDY

is an award-winning author who has written more than one hundred books for Harlequin Books. In 1995 she won Best Silhouette Romance from *RT Book Reviews* for *Anything for Danny*. In 1998 she also won a Career Achievement Award for Best Innovative Series from *RT Book Reviews*.

Carla believes the only thing better than curling up with a good book to read is sitting down at the computer with a good story to write. She's looking forward to writing many more books and bringing hours of pleasure to readers.

To my daughter, Darlene

You had no idea that your life was going to change when you woke up one morning and couldn't walk and had to go directly into a wheelchair. I know there are days you are sad and afraid, but you always manage to find your sense of humor. You'll never know how much I admire how you have handled this difficult situation. I wrote this book for you, to remind you that all things are possible and that I love you!

Chapter 1

Adam Benson sat in his pickup truck parked at the curb and stared at the two-story house out his passenger-side window. It was a nice place, painted pale beige with rust-colored trim. A large tree in the front yard sported all the colors of autumn, with bright red and orange leaves beginning to group at the base.

The Room for Rent sign had been in the front window for a couple of months, and for the past few weeks each time Adam drove by the place, he'd considered the possibility of checking it out.

Shoving a hand into the pocket of his lightweight black jacket, he found the two small plastic chips inside and rubbed them together as he considered his next move.

There was no question that he was in transition. With

two months of sobriety behind him and a ranch that no longer felt like his home, he knew it was time to make some significant changes in his life.

With a new decisiveness, he opened the truck door and got out. *Great location,* he told himself as he looked down Main Street. This house was one of the last on the block that hadn't been sold and torn down to make room for commercial property. From here he could easily walk the main drag of the small town of Grady Gulch.

He turned back to look at the house. The place had belonged to Olive Brooks for as long as he could remember. The older woman had been a fixture in town, working at the post office and involved in every charity event. Then about a year ago she'd become ill with cancer and her only daughter had come to town from someplace back east to nurse her. Olive had passed away and her daughter had remained in the house.

It was a little strange. Nobody around town that Adam had spoken to seemed to have seen Melanie Brooks since her mother's death, although he'd heard a few unpleasant rumors about her.

He jingled his sobriety chips once again. He knew personally about gossip and ugly rumors. In the past year he and his family had experienced enough of both to last a lifetime.

He finally sighed, irritated with his own hesitation. "Doesn't hurt to check it out," he muttered under his breath as he headed toward the front porch.

Next door to the house the pizza place was in full lunch swing, the scents of robust sauce and spicy sausage filling the air. Adam's stomach rumbled, and he decided that after checking out the room for rent, he'd head to the Cowboy Café for lunch. Although the pizza smelled great, at noon the place was usually overrun by high school kids grabbing a slice of pizza before their afternoon classes began.

Besides, the Cowboy Café was *the* place in town to get a hearty meal and a healthy serving of what people were saying and thinking. In the past couple of months it had felt more like home than the ranch where he'd grown up.

As he walked up the stairs to the porch, he noticed that the railing was more than a little wobbly and needed to be replaced. Up close the house paint wasn't quite as fresh as it appeared from the street. A little TLC was definitely needed, he thought, not that it was his problem. That was one of the luxuries of not owning where you lived: you weren't responsible for any of the maintenance.

He knocked on the door, and as he waited for a reply, he turned and looked back at the street where his truck was parked. Within an hour everyone in town would know that he'd been here. That was the way things worked in small towns like Grady Gulch. There were few secrets that could be sustained for any length of time.

However, there was one person in town who was keeping a dark, evil secret, a person who had murdered two women in their beds. So far law enforcement and everyone else had no idea who that killer might be and if or when he might strike again. The murders of two women who had worked as waitresses at the popular café had definitely put a gray pall over the town.

He shoved this disturbing thought aside and knocked again, this time hearing a woman's voice respond for him to hang on. The door finally opened and he got his first look at Melanie Brooks.

Stunning. She was absolutely stunning, with pale blond hair that fell to her shoulders in soft waves and eyes that were bluer than any he'd ever seen before. She was slender and wore a pair of black slacks, a black blouse and an irritated scowl that looked permanently etched onto her face. He couldn't discern how tall she might be as she sat in a wheelchair.

Adam swept his cowboy hat from his head, quickly raked his fingers through his dark hair and hoped his shock at her condition didn't show on his face. "Good afternoon. I'm Adam Benson and I'm here about the room for rent."

She blinked in obvious surprise and there was a long, awkward silence.

"You have a sign in your window? A room for rent?" he prompted.

She used her arms to move herself backward and then gestured for him to step into the foyer. "Adam Benson," she mused, her eyes narrowed as her gaze held his. "I heard you were a drunk."

Adam took a step back, stunned by her unexpected words. "I was," he admitted with painful honesty. "But I'm not drinking anymore. And the rumors I heard about you were that you're a sour, rude and cranky woman. The verdict is still out on that."

Her eyes narrowed even more. "You have a big ranch on the edge of town. Why would you need to rent a room?"

"My brother, his new wife and son have all moved into the ranch house and I'm looking for a change of address." His decision to leave the house where he'd grown up was far more complicated than that, but he figured Melanie didn't need to know the details. "So, can I see the room?"

"It's actually more than just a room. Follow me." She moved out of the foyer and into a large, airy living room with a staircase that led up to the second floor. She stopped at the foot of the staircase, the dainty frown still etched in her forehead.

For somebody who had had a sign hanging in the window for months, she seemed reluctant to allow him to see the space she was renting. Was her reluctance based on the fact that he was a male? Or was it specifically aimed at him personally? Certainly the reputation of all the Benson brothers had taken a beating in the past year, but over the past couple of months things had calmed down.

"Look, Ms. Brooks, I just need a place to hang my hat. I'm not looking for any trouble. I'll pay the rent on time and be a respectful tenant. Speaking of rent, what are you looking to get each month?"

She told him a figure that seemed a little high and he wondered if she'd done it on purpose to chase him away or if she'd intended to ask for that kind of money from anyone who showed an interest.

"Sounds good," he replied.

"I'm actually renting the entire second floor. I'm certainly not using any of the rooms upstairs." A touch of bitterness laced her voice. "Go on up and have a look around."

Adam nodded, and as he climbed the stairs, he wondered what had put her in the wheelchair. He reminded himself that it—that she—was none of his business. He was simply looking for peace and quiet, for a haven where he could gather himself together and figure out what exactly he wanted to do with the rest of his life.

The upstairs was comprised of three bedrooms and a bathroom. One of the rooms was set up like a sitting room, with a sofa, a television and an overstuffed chair with a reading lamp behind it. Adam could easily visualize himself in that big chair in the evenings, leisurely reading the newspaper or a novel.

The view from the window was of Main Street, and he stood for a moment and looked outside, trying to get a feel for the space.

The bedrooms were decorated in earth tones, making them feel neither masculine nor feminine but simply functional. The larger of the two bedrooms was located next to the sitting room and also had a view of Main Street out the window. Everything was neat and tidy and it all felt oddly right to him.

He wasn't sure what Melanie might have heard about him or his brothers, and she appeared to be the cranky sort, but surely they wouldn't have much interaction if he moved in here.

It was just a room, not a relationship, he reminded himself as he walked back down the stairs. Melanie had remained where he'd left her, at the foot of the stairs and she watched him solemnly as he hit the lower landing.

"We'd share kitchen space," she said. "You'd get the upper cabinets and I use the lower ones. You buy your own food and cook it and clean up the mess afterward." She said the words resolutely, as if she'd come to some sort of decision about him while he'd been upstairs. "It would be a month-to-month lease. I can get rid of you or you can move out with thirty days' notice. If you drink, you're out. If you're a messy pig, you're out, and if you think I'm rude or whatever, then you deal with it or move out."

He watched her closely, seeking any sign of a sense of humor lurking in her amazing blue eyes, but there didn't appear to be any. It was almost as if she were daring him to move in, confident that within thirty days he'd either want to move or she'd have a good reason to kick him out.

"I'll take it," he replied. "I'm assuming you want first and last months' rent along with a deposit of an additional month?"

She nodded. "When would you want to move in?"

"Tomorrow morning around nine?"

She released a deep sigh, although Adam couldn't tell if the sigh was of relief or apprehension. "That would be fine," she replied as she headed back toward the front door.

He followed behind her, noting how her hair shone in the sunlight that danced in through the windows. As they reached the front door, he turned and faced her once again.

Once again he was struck by her beauty. Her features were classic, high cheekbones emphasizing the slenderness of her face and her straight, perfect nose. She had a generous mouth, which might have been incredibly sexy if the corners weren't turned downward. Those lips would be inviting if she'd just smile a little bit.

For just a moment as he gazed at her, he saw a hint of vulnerability in the depths of her eyes, and a surge of unexpected protectiveness welled up inside him. How did she manage to live here by herself?

He mentally shook himself. She obviously didn't need a rescuer and that wasn't his role here. Besides, he had a feeling that if he expressed any desire to help her, she'd kick him to the curb before he'd managed to hang a shirt in one of the closets upstairs.

"Then I guess I'll see you in the morning," she said as they reached the front door. "In the meantime I'll write up an agreement for you to sign when you come back tomorrow."

"That sounds good," he replied agreeably. He started to step out on the porch but paused and turned back to her as she said his name.

"This is all new territory for me, sharing my space. I'm sure we're going to have some kinks to work out, and I forgot to tell you I don't allow music. If you must listen to a radio or whatever, then either get earphones or make sure it's low enough that I can't hear it down here."

He placed his hat back on his head and offered her a smile. "I guess we'll figure it out as we go."

It wasn't until he was back in his truck that he wondered if he'd made a mistake. Although she'd agreed to him renting the space, it was obvious she wasn't thrilled about it. And what was the deal about music? Odd. Very odd.

But the ranch house where he'd been alone for so long now once again held the sounds of a happy family. Nick, Courtney and little Garrett filled the spaces that had been empty for so long, their love lighting areas that had been full of darkness.

The truth of the matter was for the past two years Adam's heart had been filled with the darkness of loss and betrayal and shame, and he wasn't at all sure he was ready to leave that darkness behind.

His brother and his family would be better off if Adam wasn't there. They needed time to build their family without him being a third wheel.

This was the right move to make, he told himself. He clicked the two chips together in his pocket and then started the truck and pulled away from the house and headed down the street toward the Cowboy Café.

All he knew was that he needed a space of his own to figure out who he was aside from a man still grieving for the sister who had been killed in a car accident two years before, a man still fighting the desire to lose himself in the bottom of a bottle of booze.

Finally he had to come to terms with the guilt and a faint simmer of apprehension that threatened to grab him by the throat when he thought of Sam, the older brother he loved, who was currently in jail, facing charges of attempted murder.

Now Adam was moving into a house with a woman

who obviously had issues of her own. Once again he wondered what had happened to her that had placed her in a wheelchair and why nobody in town seemed to know much about Melanie Brooks despite the fact that her mother had been a resident of the small town all her life.

He frowned and reminded himself that no matter how pretty he thought she was, Melanie Brooks was a mystery he definitely didn't need to explore.

It was almost nine that evening when Melanie wheeled herself into the room that had once been a formal dining area and had been turned into a down-stairs bedroom after her mother had taken ill.

At the time of the renovation Melanie had had no idea that she was overseeing the construction of a room that would eventually become part of her own prison.

With the grace of a lame elephant she managed to pull herself up and out of the wheelchair and careen onto the bed. She straightened to a sitting position, un-dressed and then pulled her nightgown over her head and released a deep sigh of exhaustion.

She ignored the chronic tingling pain that radiated down her right leg as she reached for the lamp at the side of the bed and turned it off.

Adam Benson. She'd been surprised when he'd shown up on her doorstep, inquiring about the room, but she'd been positively stunned by an immediate, vis-ceral attraction to the long-legged cowboy.

Tilly Graves, her mother's best friend, who now came in to clean and help out three times a week, had gossiped a lot about the Benson brothers over the last couple of months, but she'd never mentioned that Adam Benson had shiny black hair with just enough curl to make a woman's fingers itch with the need to ruffle through it. Tilly had never said that Adam had blue-gray eyes with long dark lashes that a woman might covet.

Finally, Tilly had never mentioned that Adam Benson had broad shoulders, slim hips and long legs that would easily turn a woman's head in his direction.

She stared up at the dark bedroom ceiling and felt the frown that tugged her lips downward. She'd hoped to rent the rooms to a woman. That had been her goal when she'd initially hung the sign, but it had been months since then and Adam had been the first and only person to inquire about the room. Besides, the truth of the matter was that Melanie desperately needed the rent money.

It had never been her plan to be stuck here in the town she'd escaped on her high school graduation day, bringing in only a disability check that barely met minimal living expenses.

This wasn't supposed to have happened to her. She'd had a life plan since she'd been seven years old and no place in that plan had there been a wheelchair.

She closed her eyes as tears burned and the familiar taste of bitterness surged up the back of her throat. Rude? Sour and cranky? Is that really what people were whispering about her in town?

She told herself she didn't care what other people thought about her, that she had every reason to be all those things and more, but the truth of the matter was his words had stung her.

She certainly hadn't had much interaction with anyone since her mother's death. Once a week her groceries were delivered by a teenager who worked at the Shop and Go, and a month ago she'd had to contact Abe Dell, the local plumber, to take care of a leak beneath the kitchen sink. Had she been cranky with those people? *Probably,* she thought with a touch of shame. She felt as if she'd been stuck in a place of anger for a while, but surely she had good reason.

For all intents and purposes her life had ended seven months ago at the bottom of the stairs that led down to the basement. It had been exactly a week after she'd buried her mother.

Still grieving, she had been in the process of packing up some of her mother's things to donate to a local charity. She had started down the stairs to retrieve a couple of empty boxes when her foot missed a rung and plunged her into a free fall.

Melanie's right leg had been bothering her for weeks before the fall, but as a professional dancer she'd been accustomed to aches and pains for so long that she'd ignored the warning signs of unusual numbness and burning.

The fall hadn't been what had put her in the wheelchair. The stumble on the stairs had simply been a symptom of a more serious underlying condition.

She now shifted positions in the bed and consciously willed away thoughts of that day and the moment when she'd realized any dreams, any hopes she'd once had for her future had been destroyed.

She squeezed her eyes more tightly closed and sought the sweet oblivion of sleep. It didn't take long. She dreamed she was dancing, executing perfect pirouettes and leaps that suspended her in midair as music swelled in her chest, filled her soul.

Ballet, jazz and tap, she did it all and she did it well. She'd been born to dance and in her dreams she was all that she was meant to be.

The stark light of morning sunshine streaming through the nearby window pulled her from her night of happy dreams and into the glare of her harsh reality. The right foot that she'd once concentrated so hard to point had betrayed her, now dangling in a permanent point, and no matter how hard she tried, she couldn't flex it to a flat, walking position.

Peripheral neuropathy and drop foot were the official diagnoses that had put her in a wheelchair and taken away her career as a professional dancer.

For three months she'd had every neurological test there was in an attempt to find the problem and fix it, but nobody had been able to pinpoint the source of the condition, and it had been written up as lumbosacral plexopathy—nerves that didn't work right, for some unknown reason.

With the sun getting brighter and the clock reading almost eight, Melanie made the clumsy move from the bed to the wheelchair and wheeled herself into the adjoining bathroom.

Thankfully the bathroom shower was equipped with

all the special equipment it required for her to be independent. And she had to be independent. Other than Tilly there was nobody in her life and she knew the odds of having anyone else in her life on a permanent basis were minimal. She was damaged goods and would only be a burden on anyone.

It was twenty to nine when she finally left the bathroom, freshly showered and dressed in a pair of soft fleece navy blue jogging pants and a white and navy T-shirt.

She headed for the kitchen, her heart beating just a little bit faster than usual, knowing that today was the day she would start to share her house with Adam Benson.

While her emotions screamed that it was a big mistake, her logical side reminded her that renting the upstairs to him was a necessary evil. Her mother had loved this house and now it was all that Melanie had, her only security in the world. Although it had been paid off several years ago by her mother, the yearly real estate taxes would soon be due and she didn't want to give the obnoxious Craig Jenkins any opportunity to sneak in and grab the house out from under her because she couldn't afford to pay them.

She was sorry she'd ever contacted the real estate developer, but at the time she had called him, her intention had been to sell the house and get back to her dancing life in New York City as quickly as possible.

Now she had no life to return to and this house in the small Oklahoma town where she'd grown up had become her source of safety, her only real security.

It took her only minutes to fix a pot of coffee, and by the time she'd poured her first cup of the morning, a knock sounded at the door.

Nervous tension jumped in her veins as she glanced at the clock and realized it was precisely nine and her new roommate of sorts had arrived.

When she opened the door to let him in, she was once again struck by his hot handsomeness. Clad in blue jeans that hugged the length of his long legs, and in a gray T-shirt that made his eyes appear more gray than blue, he looked as if he could be a model for the quintessential cowboy.

"Good morning," he said as he swept his black hat off his head.

"Morning," she replied. "You're right on time."

He smiled at her and she felt the warmth of it deep in the pit of her stomach. "I've always thought that punctuality was a virtue." He gestured toward the curb, where a black pickup was parked. "I've got things to move in. Should I do it now, or do you want me to sign the agreement and give you a check first?"

He carried with him an energy that seemed to pulse in the air around him, an energy that seductively drew her to him. "We can take care of the business end of things after you've moved everything inside," she replied. She wheeled herself backward. "I'll be in the kitchen when you're finished."

She didn't wait for his response. Quickly pivoting her chair around, she escaped into the kitchen and moved to the table that held her cup of coffee.

Maybe it was because she'd isolated herself for the

past six months that Adam touched a chord inside her. He appeared so big, so capable, with strong shoulders that could hold the weight of the world.

Since her mother's funeral seven months ago the only people she'd seen on a regular basis were Tilly and Craig Jenkins and various doctors and nurses in Oklahoma City. Craig reminded her of a snake, with his hooded dark eyes and slender frame. Surely it wasn't any wonder that she'd react to the first attractive man who entered her small, narrow sphere.

She cast her gaze outside the window, where a light breeze stirred the trees, tugging some of the dying leaves to the ground. She'd always loved autumn, when the summer heat released its grip on the Big Apple. With her dance shoes in a canvas bag slung over her shoulder, she'd race from audition to audition with the welcome cool fall air on her face.

Now the dying leaves outside mirrored what she felt inside her soul and she had a feeling she would always hate this time of year…the time of her virtual demise.

As she heard the front door open and then close, her thoughts snapped back to Adam. A man who looked like him probably could have any woman he chose. Certainly he had a girlfriend somewhere in town.

Her heart stuttered a bit as she realized she hadn't considered that he would probably want to have guests, perhaps even female overnight guests.

She tried to imagine lying in bed at night and knowing that he was upstairs entertaining a lady. A surprising surge of envy swept through her. She told herself it had nothing to do with Adam himself but was rooted in the fact that she knew she would never again feel the comfort of a man's arms around her. She would never again enjoy the passion that a kiss could hold, experience the joy of making love.

She closed her eyes, and for just a moment she was the woman in Adam Benson's arms, she was the woman tasting his mouth, feeling his body move in unison with hers.

As she heard the front door open and close once again, she snapped out of the fantasy, irritated with herself and irrationally irritated with him.

He hadn't even finished moving his things in yet and already she had a feeling her life was about to change dramatically. She just wasn't sure if it would change for the good or the bad.

Chapter 2

It took Adam nearly an hour to get everything from the back of his pickup and to the rooms upstairs he would now call home. Deciding to unpack the boxes and clothes later in the afternoon, he went back downstairs to find Melanie and take care of the business of the new digs.

As he walked through the living room, he noticed that one of the walls was covered with photos of dancers. Funny, he'd never thought of Olive Brooks as being the type of woman to hang artsy black-and-white photos like those that adorned her wall.

It was a fleeting thought, as he found the woman in the kitchen much more of an enigma. After he'd left here the day before, he'd headed to the café. While eating lunch and chatting with the pretty owner, Mary Mathis, he'd asked what she knew about Melanie Brooks.

If anyone would have the inside scoop on anyone, it would be Mary, as the café was the social hub of the town. But she'd said that the only thing she'd heard was that Melanie lived like a hermit, never having ventured outside since her mother's funeral.

When Adam had mentioned the wheelchair, Mary had been stunned and had told Adam that at Olive's funeral a little over seven months ago Melanie had appeared healthy and perfectly capable of walking. So whatever had put her in the wheelchair was a fairly recent event.

He stepped through the threshold of the kitchen and found the object of his thoughts sitting at the table with several papers and a pen in front of her. She held a cup of coffee in her hands.

"That was fast," she said as she gestured him to one of the chairs at the round oak table.

"Actually, I just carried everything upstairs but didn't really unpack anything. I figured we'd get the paperwork out of the way first." He eased down in the chair across from her. "I thought I'd sign the papers and then, to celebrate, maybe you'd join me at the Cowboy Café for an early lunch."

She looked at him as if he'd suddenly sprouted a second head. "Thanks, but I don't go out, and besides, I think it's important that we maintain the boundaries of landlord and tenant."

"Why?" He gazed at her curiously.

"Why what?" She returned his curious gaze.

"Why don't you go out?"

"I would think it was obvious," she replied tightly as her eyes deepened to a midnight blue. "I can't walk."

He frowned thoughtfully. "I get that, but what does that have to do with you going out for a meal?"

Her mouth worked for a moment, making no sound, and then she sighed in obvious frustration. "It's too complicated for me to leave the house and in any case I don't think it's a good idea. Now, if you'll just look over these papers I drew up." She shoved two computer-printed papers across the table, along with the pen.

Adam scanned the informal agreement and saw nothing in it that raised any red flags in his mind. "Looks fine to me," he said as he grabbed the pen and signed on the line beneath where she had already signed her name.

He pushed the contract back across the table and then withdrew a check he'd written the night before from his shirt pocket. "I went ahead and wrote it for six months' worth." He leaned forward and placed the check in front of her.

"Quite the optimist, aren't you?" she said dryly.

He released a low rumble of laughter. "It's been a long time since anyone has accused me of being an optimist, but yeah, I think this arrangement is going to work out just fine."

"That makes one of us." She picked up the check and folded it in half, then tucked it into the pocket on her T-shirt.

He made her nervous, he realized as he noted the slight tremble of her hand. He'd feel better if she'd just smile…a small, simple smile. But that didn't seem to be in her repertoire of expressions.

"And now I think I'll head over to the grocery store and pick up a few items. I mostly take my meals at the Cowboy Café, but there are times I just don't feel like the company and will be eating here." He got up from the table and could almost feel the relief that coursed through her.

"I'll just remind you that the upper cabinets are all yours, and of course, you can use any space in the refrigerator that you need." She pulled back from the table a bit. "Don't you work?" she asked suddenly. "I mean, don't you have someplace you need to be every day?"

"My job has always been the family ranch, but with my younger brother back in town and taking care of things there, I've decided to take a little time off." He could tell his words didn't exactly thrill her. She was probably hoping he'd leave each day for a job and be at the house only during the evenings.

He went on. "But don't worry. I don't intend to be underfoot here." He was oddly disappointed to see an edge of relief creep into her eyes. "In fact, I'm going to get out of here right now and get those groceries."

"Before you go, I have a house key to give you." She reached into her pocket and withdrew a key. "It works on both the front and back doors."

"Thanks." He plucked it from her long, slender fingers. "And I didn't notice anything in our contract that indicated I had a curfew."

"No curfew," she replied and then shifted her gaze from him to the window. "And while I don't mind you having a guest now and then, I would prefer if you didn't have a parade of women coming in and out of the house."

He laughed again, a sharp burst of surprise. Her gaze shot back to him. "A parade of women? Hell, I haven't even had a date in over eight months. Trust me, that won't be an issue. I'm not looking for any kind of relationship right now."

Minutes later, as he drove to the nearby grocery store, he thought about her concerns regarding him and other women. He supposed he should be flattered that she thought him man enough to have a bevy of beauties at his beck and call, but the truth of the matter was Adam had never had much success with the opposite sex. Of course, he'd never tried very hard to have any kind of a relationship.

Most of his life he'd been more comfortable working with the livestock on the ranch than socializing. Recently, at thirty-three years old, Adam had come to the conclusion that he would probably live the rest of his life alone, with only the companionship of friends and extended family.

Since his oldest brother's, Sam's, arrest for attempted murder, Adam had found himself questioning what madness might lie inside himself, just waiting to spring out of nowhere.

He and Sam had been not only brothers, but also best friends, and Adam hadn't seen any of the growing madness in his brother. Somehow he'd missed important warning signals, and there were times when he lay awake in the darkness of night and wondered if that same kind of crazed madness resided someplace hidden inside him, just waiting for a trigger to release it.

He dismissed these troubling thoughts as he pulled into the parking lot of the Shop and Go, a mental list of items he wanted to buy in his head.

As he stepped into the store, the first person he saw was Sheriff Cameron Evans.

The man looked as if he'd aged ten years in the last six months, since the first waitress had been found murdered. The discovery of another body a month later had only added to the stress the sheriff had to be feeling. Thankfully for the past three months there had been no more murdered women.

"Cameron," Adam called, greeting the tall, handsome man with a somber nod. "How are you doing?"

"As well as can be expected with two cold-case murders burning a hole in my gut."

"No news on either case?" Adam asked.

Cameron shook his head and leaned forward on the handle of the shopping cart in front of him, as if the burden of the entire world weighed him down. "We've got a hundred theories, but no evidence to back up any one of them. I'm just hoping whoever killed Candy and Shirley are finished with the mini killing spree. I hope he's moved out of town and we won't lose anyone else. How is life treating you lately?"

"Good." Adam hesitated a moment and then added, "I've been attending AA meetings in Evanston once a week."

"Good for you," Cameron said with respect gleaming in his eyes.

"Thanks, and I just moved into the Brooks house. I'm renting the upper floor from Melanie."

Cameron raised an eyebrow in surprise. "What prompted that? You and Nick fighting?"

"On the contrary, things are great between me and Nick. But with him and Courtney and Garrett starting to build a real life together, I was feeling like an intruder who just happened to show up for dinner each evening. I figured it was time to give them some space and time alone. Have you met Melanie Brooks?"

"Briefly at Olive's funeral. Seemed like a nice woman. Was eager to get things taken care of here and head back to New York."

"New York? That's where she's from?" Adam asked with interest, eager to glean whatever information he could about the pretty blonde who had become his landlord.

"According to Olive, Melanie left Grady Gulch when she graduated from high school and went to New York City to become a professional dancer. Her mother was quite proud of her success. According to what she told me, Melanie had been in several Broadway musicals."

Adam was stunned by this news. "She's in a wheelchair now. I wonder what happened to her," he said, more to himself than to Cameron.

Cameron looked equally surprised. "I didn't know she was in a wheelchair. From the gossip I've heard around town, I think lots of people thought she'd left town and the house was empty. Others have said she's still grieving over her mother's death and has become a hermit. I guess she doesn't get out much. Maybe the wheelchair explains why."

Cameron shot a quick glance at his watch. "I've got to get back to the station. I'm just in here picking up some items for the guys. Jim Collins insists he makes the best Crock-Pot chili in the entire country." He flashed Adam a quick smile that momentarily alleviated the tense lines around his mouth. "We'll find out later this evening if Jim is part chef or all blowhard."

Adam laughed and the two men parted ways. As he drifted from aisle to aisle, picking up what he thought he'd need or want to eat for the next week or so, Adam's thoughts returned to Melanie.

A dancer.

She'd been a professional dancer and now she was confined to a wheelchair. Going into a wheelchair as young as she was would be difficult for anyone, but for a dancer it had to be particularly challenging.

Definitely a tragedy, he thought. What had happened to her? Was it permanent? Was it any wonder she had a reputation for being sour and bitter? Apparently life had tossed her a live grenade that had exploded and destroyed the existence she knew.

It would appear he and Melanie had more in common than he'd thought. Adam's grenade that had exploded without warning had been his brother Sam's arrest for attempted murder. When that particular bomb had detonated, it had driven Adam into a downward spiral that had ended in the bottom of a bottle of whiskey.

Nick's twenty-three-month-old son, Garrett, had

been the catalyst that had finally pulled Adam out of his self-pity and booze and back to the land of the living.

When that cute little kid looked at him with big adoring eyes and a sweet smile, Adam wanted to be the best man that he could possibly be. He didn't want to be the uncle that embarrassed the kid, who couldn't be trusted to be around him alone. Garrett had been Adam's salvation.

He knew all about raging at the unfairness of life; he understood what a cancer that rage could cause. He had a feeling whatever had happened to Melanie had cast her into an anger that could be self-destructive and could keep her isolated from all that life had to offer. As he checked out and paid for his groceries, he reminded himself that she wasn't his problem. He couldn't fix her health issues and all he really needed from her was a roof over his head.

His sole responsibility at the moment was to attend his weekly meetings in Evanston, a small town thirty minutes away. His simple goal right now was to take care of himself, to stay sober and figure out exactly who he was and where he belonged in life.

"Craig, I've told you a million times that I have no intention of selling. I'm sorry I wasted any of your time, but can't you see that my situation has changed? Why can't you just take no for an answer?" Melanie raised a hand in greeting to Adam as he entered the kitchen, laden with shopping bags.

She continued her phone conversation. "I've also asked you a dozen times to stop calling me and quit coming by here. We have no business together and I'm not going to change my mind." She didn't wait for Craig to answer, but rather slammed the phone receiver into the cradle.

"Problems?" Adam asked as he set the bags on the countertop.

Melanie moved from the telephone on the counter to the table and released a sigh of frustration. "Problems of my own making, I guess. When I first arrived back in town and realized my mother was terminally ill and her death was imminent, I contacted a real estate developer named Craig Jenkins."

Adam frowned. "A nasty piece of work. He's had a lot of business dealings here in Grady Gulch and left behind a lot of angry people. He's definitely a smooth-talking shyster."

"Yeah, well, I initially intended to take him up on an offer for the house. It's prime property for commercial business, although I thought Craig had given me a low-ball figure. Then my circumstances changed and now I'm no longer interested in selling, but Craig refuses to take no for an answer. He's become a real irritation."

Adam pulled what looked like a couple of thick steaks out of one of the grocery bags and stored them in the freezer, then turned to look at her. "The circumstance that changed is what put you in that chair?"

As always, a mention of her reality shot the taste of bitterness up the back of her throat and blew a wild wind of despair through her very bones. For a moment she couldn't speak and she simply nodded.

"I ran into Sheriff Evans in the grocery store. He told me that you were a dancer."

"I used to be a dancer," she replied, the bitterness sneaking in to lace her words.

"According to Cameron you were a successful working dancer." He continued to unload the groceries he'd bought.

"I was." Why was he asking her about it? Didn't he realize the entire subject was painful to her?

He turned from the freezer door and his gaze was dark, sympathetic, as it lingered on her. She hated that. She hated his sympathy.

"But that was then and this is now," she said with a lift of her chin.

"So what happened?" He closed the freezer door and leaned against it with his back.

"The official diagnosis is drop foot and peripheral neuropathy and a bunch of other doctor jargon. In other words my brain isn't speaking to my right leg and foot and the nerves have all gone crazy. I've been to a dozen neurologists and been tested for everything from multiple sclerosis to diabetes, but none of them were able to find the source of the problem. So it is what it is." The bitterness was back in her voice.

"Can it be fixed?"

"I've been told to learn how to live with it." "Just shut up about it," she wanted to tell him, but instead she bit her lower lip.

He seemed to be attempting to look inside her soul, and she broke eye contact with him, not wanting to see any more sympathy in the depths of his eyes. She had enough self-pity. She didn't need anyone else's.

"Tough break," he replied.

"Yes, it was. And now, if you'll excuse me, I'm feeling a bit tired. I'm going to lie down for a while."

With a need to escape whatever further conversation he'd planned to have with her, she scooted out of the room and into her bedroom, where she closed the door as tears stung her eyes.

The phone call from Craig had upset her and she felt too fragile to have any meaningful discussion about her life in a wheelchair. There was nothing to discuss.

She was in a wheelchair and therefore had no life.

She wheeled herself over to the window and stared out at the backyard. She'd spent most of her childhood and teenage years in the yard, practicing leaps, stretching for a perfect arabesque, and dreaming about the big lights and city streets of New York.

She'd had a small group of friends in high school, but none of them had understood her drive to succeed, to leave the small town and make a life doing what she loved. They had talked about getting married and having children, becoming hairdressers or schoolteachers right here in Grady Gulch.

Her mother used to joke that she'd come out of the womb dancing. Dancing wasn't just something Melanie had done; it had been the sum of her being. And she didn't know how to *be* without it.

She hadn't seen any of her old friends since returning to town. Initially she'd been too busy nursing her mother for any kind of social life. Besides, she hadn't seen the point in renewing old acquaintances since her intention was to bury her mother and head back to New York.

Now she didn't want to see any of those old friends or anyone else in town. They would all look at her with pity and she couldn't handle that.

Thankfully she didn't have to worry about having any more intimate discussions with Adam. After she'd napped, she returned to the kitchen and heard no noise from the upstairs. A glance out the front window let her know Adam's truck was gone, so he wasn't home.

It was ridiculous, the kind of tension his very presence wrought inside her. She was far too aware of him as a sexy male, when she needed to look at him objectively like the cash cow that was going to save her house.

Still, it was hard to stay objective when he focused those gorgeous eyes on her, when the clean male scent of him eddied in the air around her and his energy filled the corners of the room.

She was twenty-eight years old, and her reaction to Adam reminded her that although her leg and foot were dead, apparently her hormones were not. Not that it mattered.

She spent the remainder of the evening watching television in the living room and then at nine o'clock once again went into her bedroom to prepare for bed.

As she got into her midnight-blue silk nightgown, she wondered where Adam was and who he might be with. *None of your business,* a little voice whispered in the back of her brain.

He was just a tenant, renting a couple of rooms. He had a life of his own and what he did, where he went had absolutely nothing to do with her. She had to somehow figure out how to rebuild her life without dance, without her mother for support.

As she lay in the dark, her thoughts drifted to her mother. How she missed her. She'd scarcely had time to grieve for her before the fall down the stairs. Now what she'd like more than anything was to hear her mother's laughter, see her beloved face wreathed with a smile one last time.

How she wished she could hear her mother tell her that everything was going to be all right, that Melanie was strong enough to get through anything.

Olive had been Melanie's rock, a no-nonsense woman who had, despite her better judgment, bought into Melanie's dreams of dancing and had believed in her talent. Olive had worked all day at the post office and then had often taken other part-time jobs to make sure Melanie could continue with her dance lessons.

After Melanie had moved to New York, she and her mother had talked on the phone nearly every day. Melanie would get care packages from her mother with baked cookies and fuzzy socks and a little hard-earned cash tucked into an envelope. After several years of working, it was Melanie's turn to send envelopes with extra cash to her mother.

She wished her mother was here right now, to tell her to suck it up, to quit whining about lemons and get to work making lemonade.

Olive had never been the type to indulge in any kind

of self-pity. She was the strongest woman Melanie had ever known. Even when her husband had walked out on them when Melanie was two, Olive had tamped down her sadness and resentment. She had sucked back her tears and had set to work to build the best life she could for herself and her daughter.

Since her mother's death and with the onslaught of her medical condition, Melanie had never felt so alone. She told herself again and again that she didn't want anyone in her life. She was perfectly capable of taking care of herself, and she didn't want to need anyone, because she was certain there would never be anyone there for her.

Still, when she heard the front door open and then close just after ten and the sound of Adam's footsteps heading up the stairs, a strange sense of security filled her. She realized that at least for the rest of the night she was no longer alone.

He stood beneath the big maple tree in her front yard. Around him the darkness was complete; even the stars and the moon were hidden beneath a thick veil of clouds. At one in the morning even the dogs and cats of Grady Gulch didn't stir.

It was his favorite time to stand and look at the house and think of *her*.

Melanie.

Her name was a pressure tight inside his chest, half choking his breath from his body. It rang in his ears with a discordant chime that hurt his head.

She didn't belong here.

He clenched his fists tightly as a surge of anger threatened to drive all reasonable thoughts from his head. What he wanted to do right now was break through her front door, take her from her bed and punish her.

It wasn't enough that fate had already chastised her for her ambition by putting her in the wheelchair. She deserved more punishment...so much more.

It would be so easy to gaslight her, make her think she was losing her mind. He clapped a hand over his mouth to halt a burst of laughter that threatened to escape at the very thought.

He could drive her a little crazy, make her doubt her own sanity and then take her and punish her for all her sins for good.

He should have taken her last night or the night before. He'd had no idea that somebody would appear to rent part of her house. That complicated things.

Still, he was a patient man, and he knew that if he watched and waited long enough, the perfect opportunity would present itself.

He slowly uncurled his fists and drew a deep breath of the cool night air. As he moved away from the house, he was reminded that autumn was the time of death. He wouldn't be satisfied until Melanie Brooks was as dead as the leaves that crunched beneath his feet.

Chapter 3

A shrill scream pulled Melanie from her bed the next morning. In a panic she jumped into the wheelchair and left her bedroom, only to see Tilly racing down the stairway wielding a feather duster as a weapon, followed by a dripping wet Adam with just a towel wrapped around his waist.

"It's okay, I live here!" Adam exclaimed as he chased the frightened woman down the staircase. He spied Melanie and halted, obvious relief on his face. "Tell her," he said to Melanie. "Tell her I'm not some crazy serial killer hiding out in a shower stall."

"Adam is renting the upstairs," Melanie replied, surprised to feel her mouth threatening to stretch into a grin.

Tilly sprawled on a nearby chair with a hand to her

heart, her wrinkled face still holding the remnants of horror. "I went up to dust the rooms and he stepped out of the bathroom and I thought for sure he was going to kill me."

"What did you think he was going to do? Flip you to death with the end of his towel?" A giggle escaped Melanie as Adam's cheeks flooded with color.

"I'll just go back upstairs and get dressed." He backed up the stairs, as if afraid by turning around, his bare tush might show.

Melanie had no doubt it was a fine tush, and for the first time since she'd returned to Grady Gulch, she released a full belly laugh. It felt good. It felt so darned good after so many months of having nothing to laugh about.

Tilly looked at her in surprise and then straightened up on the chair. "Well, I'm certainly glad you find it funny. You might have warned me that Adam Benson had moved in here."

"He just moved in yesterday, so I haven't had a chance." Melanie tried to erase the vision she'd just had of Adam, but it was proving difficult.

His broad chest was fully muscled and his abdomen above the towel was a perfect six-pack. His long legs were sturdy and masculine in shape and for a moment the sight of him had halted Melanie's ability to breathe.

"Are you sure renting the rooms to him is something you want to do?" Tilly asked, worry darkening her hazel eyes.

"It's something I have to do," she replied. "Tilly, you know my situation. Mom's estate left me nothing ex-

cept the house and I was living paycheck to paycheck
in New York. I need some extra cash coming in and
Adam was the only person who came to see the rooms.
I've had that For Rent sign in the window for months."

Tilly glanced up the stairs, where he'd disappeared.
"Talk around town is that he's cleaned up his act, but
if he gives you any trouble, you just say the word and
I'll kick him to the curb for you." To demonstrate her
intentions, she stood and kicked out one skinny leg,
which might move a gnat but certainly not a man as
big, as built as Adam.

"Oh, Tilly, I don't know what I'd do without you!"
Melanie exclaimed in a burst of gratitude.

Tilly walked over to her and planted a kiss on top
of her head. "You'd do fine without me. You're brave
and strong, but in any case I like doing things for you.
Your mother was my very best friend in the world and
she'd roll over in her grave if I didn't do what I could
to help you."

She cupped Melanie's face with her hands. "You're
the daughter I never had. Olive shared you with me."
She straightened. "And now I'm going into the kitchen
to make you a big breakfast. If that man wants to eat,
then I'll make enough for all of us."

"I imagine he'll want to eat," Melanie called after
her as the skinny Tilly walked purposely toward the
kitchen.

When she was gone, Melanie thought of that moment
of laughter that had spilled out of her. It had felt good.
She used to laugh a lot, but the laughter had been stolen
from her at the same time that dance had been taken.

She couldn't get her dance back, but maybe it was time she tried to get a little bit of laughter and fun back in her life.

She suddenly realized that she'd shot out of bed so quickly at the sound of Tilly's scream that she was still clad in the silk nightgown that clung to her naked curves.

Hopefully Adam had been too concerned about his own half nakedness to have noticed hers. By the time she changed into a pair of jeans and a T-shirt and returned to the living room, the scent of fried bacon filled the house.

As if pulled by the savory scent alone, Adam came down the stairs, this time fully dressed in jeans and a gray T-shirt.

He cast her a sheepish grin. "I'm a little more presentable now, but I've got to admit she scared me as much as I frightened her. I didn't realize Tilly was a friend of yours. She used to help out at our ranch with some occasional cleaning. Thank God those are big bath towels."

A new giggle escaped Melanie's lips and she slapped her hand across her mouth to stifle it.

"Don't," he said, his eyes lighting up with humor. "Don't stifle that laugh. I've been waiting since last night just to see a smile on you."

The humor died as she pulled her hand from her mouth. "I haven't had much to smile about over the last few months."

She watched as he walked over to the wall of pictures. They had been her mother's trophies, her motherly pride displayed in black and white.

"These are all of you," he said, his voice holding a hint of surprise.

She nodded. "Whenever I got a new gig dancing, I'd send my mom a photo of me in my costume," she explained. "I always had them done in black and white because mom said the color took away from the beauty of my pose." She didn't like to look at the photos now. They were simply painful reminders of what, of who she was no longer.

"They're beautiful," he said as he moved from photo to photo. "You loved it, didn't you?" He turned back to look at her and she nodded. "It shows. It's in every line of your body, shining from your eyes."

"And now it's all gone," she replied flatly.

"It's tough when good things disappear." He sat in the chair Tilly had recently vacated. "Have you decided what you're going to do now?"

"I guess I'm going to sit in this chair for the rest of my life." The bitterness was back, and even though she tried to bite it back, she knew he heard it ringing in her voice.

"Surely you had other dreams when you were young," he said gently.

"None that I can remember," she said sharply. He was treading into private territory. He was a tenant, not a friend, and she barely knew him at that.

"I happened to run into one of your friends last night." It was obvious by his change in topic that he'd realized he'd veered too close for comfort.

"One of my friends?"

"Once a week I drive into Evanston to attend an AA meeting and that's where I went last night and I just happened to run into Craig Jenkins."

She looked at him in surprise. "Craig was at an AA meeting?"

"No, he was working late in his realty office. I just stopped by and let him know I was staying here with you now and reminded him that you weren't interested in selling and that it was out of line for him to keep bothering you."

"Did you say it just like that?" she asked.

The corner of his mouth turned up in a sexy grin. "I might have used a few more forceful words. You were just so upset when you were talking to him on the phone yesterday. Did I overstep my boundaries?" he asked worriedly.

"No...and thank you." A wave of gratefulness swept over her. He had to have gone out of his way to confront Craig and she knew he'd done it solely for her peace of mind.

"Breakfast is ready," Tilly called from the kitchen.

"You want to join me?" Melanie asked.

He flashed her a smile of pleasure. "I'd intended to go to the Cowboy Café for breakfast, but your offer is much nicer."

He stood and she was acutely conscious of him behind her as she wheeled herself into the kitchen and into the spot at the table that was absent a chair.

"We've got eggs and bacon and pancakes," Tilly said as she bustled to get the food to the table.

Adam sank down in the chair opposite Melanie. "Sorry I scared you, Tilly," he said.

"So you two know each other?" Melanie asked. "Adam told me you used to do a little housekeeping for his family."

"I was a good friend of Adam's mother, God rest her soul, and after her death Sam occasionally had me come in and do a little cleaning." She pointed a spatula at Adam. "And you were always the messiest of the bunch."

Adam grinned and as usual Melanie found his smile warm and inviting. "I promise I've grown up since then, Tilly. My dirty socks always manage to find their way into the clothes hamper these days."

Tilly snorted, set a plate before each of them and then looked at Melanie. "I'm going to dust upstairs now that I know there aren't any half-naked men lurking around. I'll be back down shortly."

Melanie and Adam exchanged amused glances as Tilly left the room.

"She been working for you long?" he asked as he poured a liberal amount of syrup over his pancakes.

"She doesn't exactly work for me. She was best friends with my mother, and I think before my mother died, she asked Tilly to see after me. Of course, at that time neither my mother nor Tilly had any idea that I'd be in a wheelchair within a week." Melanie reached for a slice of toast that was on a small plate in the center of the table.

"I'm not sure what I would have done without Tilly in the first months when I couldn't walk. She drove me to Oklahoma City for doctors' appointments, made sure I had food to eat and held me whenever I couldn't hold back my tears. She's been a godsend, although I'm learning each day to be more independent. I don't want to be a burden on anyone, and even though I've tried to tell her I don't need her coming over here three or four times a week, she insists."

"She loves you," Adam observed.

"Love shouldn't be so much work for one person," she replied dryly. She cast her gaze out the window. "Looks like it's going to be a beautiful day," she said in an effort to change the topic to something more neutral.

"The last couple of days have been gorgeous. Autumn is one of my favorite times of year. The air outside smells different than it does at any other time… with a hint of woodsmoke and apples. If the weather stays this nice the trick-or-treaters will be out in full force at the end of the month."

Melanie found herself relaxing as the conversation turned to Halloweens past. Adam told her about one year when his brother and sister decided to put together a haunted farm for people to visit.

"It was a disaster," he admitted with a grin. "We cut a maze through an old cornfield but forgot to cut an exit out of it. Cherry was supposed to play a dead victim, but every time a cute boy came in, she'd jump up to flirt with him." Adam laughed and shook his head. "I think we scared ourselves while we were setting it up more than we scared anyone who eventually came through it."

In turn Melanie told him about fall in New York City,

how the colors in Central Park could take your breath away and the street vendors added apple cider and cinnamon and caramel apples to their wares. She'd loved Central Park in the fall.

Normal. For the first time in seven months she felt normal, enjoying an easy conversation with a handsome man while eating breakfast.

She heard the sound of Tilly turning on the vacuum in her bedroom, the sound background noise as Adam continued to regale her with stories from his past.

It was only when the meal was finished and he stood and grabbed her plate to clear the table that tension surged up inside her and the reality of the situation hit home.

"I can clear my own dishes," she said with more force than necessary.

"Sorry. Just trying to help," he replied as he pulled his hand back and instead grabbed his own plate.

"I don't need any help." She heard the sharpness of her voice but seemed unable to rein it in. By his simple action of attempting to help her, he'd shattered the momentary feeling of normalcy. He'd reminded her that she was inadequate, that she was in a wheelchair.

She sat still, hating herself, as Adam cleared his plate and silverware. When he'd finished, he turned and looked at her, his eyes dark and hooded. "I'm heading out for a while. I'll be back later."

He didn't wait for her response but rather turned on his heels and headed for the front door. Melanie winced as she heard the door open and then close behind him, leaving her alone in the kitchen.

Alone.

As she was meant to be. Alone, as she always would be. If her disability didn't chase people out of her life, then certainly her attitude would. She couldn't do anything about being in a wheelchair, but she was growing sick of her own attitude. Maybe it was time to change, to somehow look forward and discover something new she could do, instead of dwelling on all the things she could no longer accomplish.

It was a new mind-set for her and just a little bit frightening. For the past seven months she'd clung to her anger and bitterness at life and without it she wasn't sure who she would be, but she knew for a fact she didn't want to be the way some of the people in town had characterized her.

Somehow, someway, she had to figure out how to put her anger aside and find acceptance, but the one thing she was determined to do was not fall for the cowboy who now lived under her roof. That would just be asking for heartache.

"She's definitely a prickly sort," Adam said to his brother Nick as the two sat at his kitchen table. Garrett sat in his high chair, eating the last of a bowl of mac and cheese, and Courtney was at the sink, putting the remaining lunch dishes into the dishwasher.

Adam had been living in the Brooks house for three days, and since their shared breakfast, Melanie had been particularly aloof. They'd eaten at different times, and she'd spent most of her days and nights in her bedroom, as if actively avoiding his company.

Tilly had told him she had a computer in her room and spent a lot of time surfing the Internet, ordering items she needed and doodling on a sketch pad. For a woman as beautiful as her, her self-isolation felt like a new tragedy.

"I feel bad for her. It must be tough to have so much taken away from you, especially at such a young age." Courtney, Nick's wife, moved to the table with three glasses of iced tea. She cast a glance at Nick. "I know how hard it is to let go of bitterness."

Nick looked chagrined. When Nick had left Grady Gulch after their sister's death, he hadn't realized he'd left his girlfriend, Courtney, pregnant. He'd been gone a little over two years when Sam was arrested, and Adam had become a drunk, and so Nick had decided to come home to help sort things out. Nick and Courtney had reconnected and had married a month ago in a small ceremony where little Garrett as ring bearer had nearly eaten the rings.

"She's gorgeous and smart and yet at twenty-eight years old she's holed herself up in that house, just waiting for death to eventually come," Adam replied. "She's completely given up on herself and life."

"Is it possible somebody has a little crush on the pretty woman in the wheelchair?" Courtney asked in a teasing tone.

Adam laughed and hoped the heat in his cheeks didn't show outwardly. "I'm not even sure she likes me very much. I think she just puts up with me because she needs the rent money to help pay off some back taxes she owes on the house."

"It's got to be tough, though, to be so young and facing the rest of her life in a wheelchair," Courtney replied. "She's got to be suffering from some depression."

"True, but being in a wheelchair isn't a death sentence," Adam replied. "She should be getting out of that house, enjoying the feel of the sun on her face, the wind in her hair."

"You should know better than anyone that you can't make somebody do something if they aren't willing," Nick chided. Adam knew Nick was thinking about the first couple of days after he returned to the ranch, when he tried to get Adam to quit drinking.

"Yeah, but she spends a lot of time looking out the window, like she wants to get out but is afraid or something," Adam said.

"Does she have a way out?" Courtney asked. "The Brooks house isn't exactly handicap friendly with the stairs coming off the porch. How does she manage inside the house?"

"Quite well. Tilly Albright comes in a couple times a week to do some cleaning and cooking, but for the most part Melanie seems relatively self-sufficient inside the house," Adam replied. He took a sip of his iced tea and thought about the past three days.

It was as if he and Melanie had warily circled each other, careful not to step on each other's toes or get too personal. For Adam the days had been particularly hard as he'd fought against a growing respect and the faint thrum of an unexpected desire for her.

It had begun on the morning he'd frightened Tilly and raced down the stairs to explain to her that she knew him and he wasn't the serial killer haunting the town. He'd been embarrassed to find himself on the stairs clad only in a towel, but he'd been enchanted when he'd seen Melanie in her dark blue nightgown.

The spaghetti straps had exposed her slender shoulders, the silk material had hugged her curves and the plunging neckline had given him a glimpse of the grace of her long neck and the creamy skin of the top of her small breasts.

He never really considered a real relationship with a woman before. He definitely knew he wasn't in a place in his life to have anything to offer to a woman. With two months' sobriety behind him and a need to figure himself out, the last thing he needed to do was drag a woman into the uncertainty of his own life.

"Unc Dam!" Garrett exclaimed and with his cheesy finger pointed at Adam and smiled.

"Uncle Adam loves you," Adam replied and leaned over to kiss the boy on his dark hair.

"He misses having you here," Nick said.

"It's better this way," Adam replied. "I needed my own space and so did the three of you."

"You coming back to work on the ranch?" Nick asked.

"Only if you really need me. You were always the real rancher around here. I'm trying to figure out what I want to do with the rest of my life."

Nick smiled at him. "Anything we can do to help?"

"Nah, I think I need to suffer through this early midlife crisis all alone," Adam responded.

"If you trade your truck in for some fancy little

sports car, then we're stepping in," Courtney said, making them all laugh.

A half an hour later, as he drove past the lumber store, part of his conversation with his brother and sister-in-law still lingered in his head. On impulse he turned into the parking lot.

When he'd asked Melanie why she didn't go out, she'd said it was complicated. Hell yes, it was complicated without a ramp. He could only assume that when she went out to doctors' appointments, she'd have to leave the house by the back door and go through the side yard and around to the front of the house to get into Tilly's car.

Minutes later, as he helped load the lumber and nails he'd just bought on the back of his truck, he knew that he was definitely overstepping his boundaries and he also knew he was running the risk of majorly ticking off Melanie. But the truth of the matter was he wanted more for her than she seemingly wanted for herself.

Funny, for the last couple of months Adam had done nothing but look inward and feel sorry for himself. It felt good to actually do something for somebody else.

He had no idea if she'd really use the ramp he intended to build, but he liked the idea that if she decided to venture outside, he was making it a little easier for her.

He arrived back at the house just after two, lumber and tools loaded in the back of his truck. He didn't go inside to tell her his intentions. He decided it would be easier to beg forgiveness than to ask for permission.

He'd just started hammering the nails in the frame

when the front door opened and Melanie appeared at the threshold. "What on earth are you doing?" she asked.

He straightened and eyed her boldly. "Probably overstepping my boundaries." He knew she possibly wouldn't be happy, and she didn't disappoint him. Her nostrils thinned and Adam steeled himself for whatever was about to come.

"What are you doing?" she repeated.

"I'm building a ramp."

"Why?" There was an unmistakable belligerence in her voice.

He thought she'd never looked so gorgeous, sitting so straight and tall in the chair, with her bright blue eyes blazing.

"Because you need one." He picked up a nail and hammered it into the wood, acutely aware of her continuing to glare at him.

"I'm not reimbursing you for whatever you spent on such nonsense," she yelled to be heard over his pounding.

He stopped hammering and straightened up once again to look at her. "I didn't intend for you to. I just figured if you had to get out of the house, say, in the case of an emergency, a ramp would make it possible. From the end of the wood you have nice sidewalks that will take you anyplace you want to go in town."

"I don't want to go anyplace in town!" she exclaimed and then backed up and slammed the door to punctuate her sentence.

Her response didn't deter him from the task at hand. It took him a little over two hours to build an adequate ramp and finish it off with strips of nonskid material, which he placed every twelve inches to assure her safety in the rain or snow.

When he was done, he leaned back against the side of his truck and looked at the work. He was satisfied. The ramp was solid and wide enough and had a gentle slope that would make it easy for her to maneuver in the chair. *If* she ever decided to try it, he thought ruefully. Eventually, if she wanted, he'd put up solid railings on either side.

He cleaned up his tools and stored them in the back of his truck and then went inside and up the stairs to shower and change clothes. As he passed through to the stairs, there was no sign of Melanie. She'd probably retreated to her room to have a private temper fit.

At least she hadn't asked him to stop building or to tear down what he'd done, he thought as he stepped into the shower spray.

He'd heard her laughter only once and it was a beautiful sound that he wished he heard more often. She broke his heart just a little bit, not because she was in a wheelchair, but rather because she had decided to stop living.

Just like Adam had done when Sam was arrested. Yes, Adam knew all about hiding from life, denying a reality too painful to endure.

But what he was slowly discovering was that sometimes you just had to adjust your expectations of the way you thought your life should go and grab onto happiness wherever and whenever it could be found.

Sick of his mental journey into the philosophy of

life, he got out of the shower, dressed in a pair of clean jeans and a long-sleeved button-up shirt and headed downstairs to face the music.

Music. Funny that she didn't want the sound of music in the house. It was a fleeting thought as he found her in the living room, at the window, staring out at his masterpiece.

"It looks steep," she said, her voice just short of grumpy.

"It's not at all."

She turned around to look at him and her eyes were a troubled midnight blue. "I don't want to go out. I don't want to see people. When I left here, I bragged about all the things I was going to do…. I was going to be a professional dancer and work on Broadway, and now I'm back where I started and a complete failure."

Adam pointed to the pictures hanging on the wall. "That's not failure," he replied. "That's success. You did what you set out to do and then you suffered a physical injury. You're like a football player who won the Super Bowl but then blew out his knee and can never play again. It's simply time to readjust your goals."

She looked down at her hands in her lap. "I don't want to see the pity in people's eyes."

Adam walked over to her and crouched down in front of her. He could smell her, a seductive scent of spice and floral that momentarily dizzied his senses. His heart banged as he reached out and took one of her hands in his.

Dainty and cold, it lay lifeless in his own, but he was shocked by the electric connection that sizzled through him at the simple touch.

"People will only look at you with pity if you're pitiful," he said. "There's a man here in town, Brandon Williams. He's a war veteran, and his face is scarred, he's bald and he's in one of those motorized wheelchairs. He runs all around town. He's pleasant and has a great sense of humor, and nobody feels sorry for him, because he obviously doesn't feel sorry for himself."

Her hand slowly warmed and tightened in his. "But I do feel sorry for myself." She offered him a small smile. "And I'm getting pretty sick of it, of myself."

"Then have dinner with me at the Cowboy Café tonight. Let people see that you're in a wheelchair, but you're just fine. Let them know that you're dealing with the injury that sidelined you from your very successful career."

His desire to take her out was palpable in the air as she squeezed his hand even more tightly. He knew he was way too invested in getting her out of the house, out around people who might help her transition into a less lonely existence.

She hesitated for a long moment and then nodded. "Okay," she finally replied softly.

"Great!" he exclaimed. He gave her hand an answering squeeze and then released it and stood. "Why don't we plan on heading out of here in about an hour? That will get us to the café around six."

"I'm nervous," she admitted and her lower lip trembled slightly.

"There's no need to be nervous. The people of this town are good people. Besides, I'll be right beside you the whole night and I would never let anything bad happen to you." As he said the words forcefully, he realized that Melanie Brooks was definitely getting under his skin and he wasn't sure that was necessarily a good thing.

Chapter 4

Myriad emotions whirled through Melanie as she dressed for the dinner out with Adam. There was no question that she was nervous about facing people, but there was also something about him that made her more than a little bit nervous.

She stared at the mirror, and instead of seeing a reflection of herself, she saw herself as she'd once been. The young woman in the mirror was clad in a red costume that sparkled in the stage lights.

She closed her eyes and raised her face as if to seek the warmth of a spotlight. She was comfortable there in the heat of the glare, and the dancer in her mind began to move, raising her leg behind her in a perfect arabesque. The beautiful ballet movement was followed by quick jazz steps that led into more classic ballet.

The music of the dance swelled in her soul, tingled throughout her body and thrummed in her heart. She soared across the stage in leaps, executed perfect battements and developpes. She was one with the music. Her body responded in movement to the beat of the drums, to the throaty voice of a saxophone, to the trill of clarinets, all coming together in an orchestra of beauty.

The audience roared their approval as she finally came to the end of the dance and curtsied.

She opened her eyes and stared at her reflection, shocked to find herself a woman with runny mascara seated in a wheelchair. *A ridiculous flight of fancy,* she told herself as she hurriedly fixed her makeup. Adam was waiting for her and she was wasting time trapped in the past, remembering who she'd once been.

With her face once again in order, she wheeled out of the bathroom and her bedroom to find him standing at the front door.

"Ready?" he asked with an encouraging smile.

"As ready as I'm going to get," she replied.

Adam took her outside and down the ramp to the sidewalk. Logically she knew she couldn't hide out in the house forever, and she certainly couldn't spend all her time lost in the past. Still, emotionally, she wasn't at all sure she was ready to face anyone.

She ran nervous fingers down the front of the royal blue blouse she'd paired with some navy slacks. She'd actually put on not only mascara but also a touch of pink lipstick for the first time in months for the outing.

"I can take it from here," she said to Adam when

they reached the bottom of the ramp and moved onto the smooth sidewalk.

He let go of the wheelchair handles and stepped beside her. "Are you sure?"

She nodded. "I like to manually wheel myself. It keeps my upper body strong and fit."

"How are you feeling mentally?" he asked as they headed down the sidewalk toward the café in the distance.

"A little scared, but I also know it's past time I get out of the house. I've had seven months to mourn and be angry at the blow fate gave me. I'm tired of my own company and sick of my self-pity."

"That's the first sign of getting better," he replied. "When Sam got arrested for attempting to kill Lizzy Wiles, I fell into a well of self-pity that had me hitting the bottle hard. I made a fool of myself a hundred times, wound up in places I didn't remember going and felt like hell. I finally got tired of being sick and tired and decided to make some changes."

"Were you always a drinker?" she asked, anxious to think about anything but the café in the distance.

"No, never." He shoved his hands in his pockets, a habit she'd noticed he did frequently. "I'm not an alcoholic, although I go to the meetings because I like the camaraderie I've found there. I went to a very dark place with Sam's arrest, but alcohol was never an issue before then and hasn't been an issue since I decided to stop drinking."

"So what are your plans for your future?" she asked, trying to still the nerves that pirouetted in the pit of her stomach. "I've noticed you aren't working at your ranch."

"I'm thinking about maybe talking to Cameron about something in law enforcement."

"Really?" She looked up at him in surprise. "That's quite a stretch from a rancher."

He smiled down at her. "Yeah, but I'm ready for a new chapter in my life and I've always had a bit of interest in crime solving and peacekeeping."

She looked toward the café. "You're forcing me to be ready for a new chapter in my life."

He laughed. "I'm not the one who changed into that pretty blouse that makes your eyes look gorgeous and your hair shine like an angel's." His cheeks dusted with color, he averted his gaze from hers. "I don't want to force you to do anything, Melanie. I just want good things for you."

A flutter of warmth swept through her. Was he flirting with her with all those lovely words? *Ridiculous,* she told herself. Why would a healthy, vital man like Adam flirt with somebody like her?

He was just being kind to the crippled girl, she told herself. He probably helped old ladies across the street and nursed sick dogs back to health.

Adam was the type of man who would eventually find a woman who could stand beside him, give him children, and play an active role as wife and mother. She might have been that kind of woman once, but no longer.

Once again her nerves grew taut as they drew close enough to the café that she could smell the wonderful scents that filled the air, see the people getting out of cars and heading for the front door. As a full onslaught of nerves struck her, her arms quit moving and the wheelchair came to a halt.

"Tired?" Adam asked. "I'd be glad to push you the rest of the way."

"No, I'm fine. I just need a minute." She drew in a deep breath and released it slowly, just like she used to do before she'd go onstage.

"You said you went to school here, that you once had friends. Don't you think those people will be thrilled to see you again?" Adam asked.

"Maybe," she replied tentatively. She drew another breath and then began to turn the wheels to move her forward once again. "It's been a long time since I left Grady Gulch. I'm sure there are lots of people here now that I don't even know."

"I'll introduce you and you'll never eat better food than what Mary Mathis offers at the café."

"Mary Mathis? I think I met her at my mother's funeral. A pretty blonde?"

"That's Mary," Adam agreed. "She's a widow who moved here with her son about eight years ago. Five years ago she bought the café. Melanie, if you really want to make your life here, then all you have to do is open your heart up and the people of Grady Gulch will welcome you with open arms."

Within five minutes of entering the establishment, that was exactly what Melanie discovered. Adam led her to a table for two and quickly dispensed with one of the chairs, allowing her to wheel right up.

She was acutely aware of gazes following her progress, but as Adam sat in the seat across from her, she knew she was going to get through this first outing just fine.

Before they'd even placed their orders, people began to stop by the table to say hello and many of them were old friends of Melanie's.

The first person who ambled to the table was Denver Walton, a boy Melanie had dated briefly in high school. "Hey, Melanie. I didn't know you were back in town," he said. "Wow. What happened to you?"

Adam spoke up. "It's a work-related injury. You know she was a dancer on Broadway."

"Yeah…yeah, I heard that. I always knew you'd do something great with your dancing. So are you in town to stay?" He shot a quick glance over his shoulder to Maddy Billings, who sat in a nearby booth and glared at Melanie.

Some things never changed, Melanie thought with a touch of humor. Maddy had hated Melanie in high school and it looked like that was still the case after all these years.

"Hey, maybe sometime we could meet up for coffee or something, you know, talk about old times," Denver said. "You can tell me all about your time in the big city."

The invitation surprised her and she murmured something non-committal and was grateful the waitress had arrived to take their orders. Denver returned to his booth, rejoining seething blond-haired, attractive Maddy.

Denver wasn't the only old friend she saw as they waited for their meal to be delivered. Deputy Jim Collins came by to tell her hello, as did half a dozen women she'd run around with when they were all teenagers.

The women all screamed and giggled like the young girls they had once been, and promises were made to call, to plan lunch and get together for a real girls-only reunion.

With each minute that passed, with every person she spoke to, she began to relax more and more. Maybe there was life after wheelchair death. Maybe she'd been attempting to pull the grave dirt over her face far too soon.

She didn't know what the future held, but at the moment she was satisfied to be sitting in the Cowboy Café, across from a man who made her heart beat just a little too fast in her chest.

"Here we are." The waitress with a name tag that read Lynette set their plates in front of them. Melanie's stomach rumbled as she gazed down at the chicken fried steak with mashed potatoes and gravy.

"This is positively sinful."

"You should eat," Adam said. "You look like a puff of smoke might blow you away."

"I've always been thin, which was a good thing as a dancer," she replied. "My friends who were also dancers hated that I could pretty much eat anything I wanted and never put on any weight."

"Must have been a tough life, trying to make it on-stage in New York City."

"It was tough," she agreed. "It was heartbreaking

and exhilarating. It was the best and worst of times and I loved it." For a moment the grief threatened to take hold of her, but she swallowed against it, refusing to allow the evening to be ruined by all that had been lost.

"Everyone always thinks about the glamour of being a dancer on Broadway, but the truth was I shared an apartment the size of a postage stamp with two other girls. Most nights we were soaking our feet or bandaging bleeding toes. We pooled our money to buy Bengay by the gallon and it was a luxury if we could afford to order a pizza every couple of weeks."

"It sounds awful."

Melanie laughed. "It does, doesn't it? But none of the bad stuff mattered once the music began and the spotlights came on." She took a bite of her potatoes. "Now, tell me everything there is to know about Adam Benson."

He grinned. "I'm not sure the meal will be long enough."

She tried to focus on the conversation as he told her about his parents dying when they were young and Sam getting custody and keeping the family together at the ranch, but it was hard to focus on his words when she wanted to fall into the soft blue of his eyes.

As she'd watched from the window as he built the ramp, she'd wanted to be mad at him for his presumptuousness, but instead something bitter had broken inside her.

What she felt now was a fragile, tentative hope that she hadn't felt for months…the hope that she could get back some semblance of a life, and it was all due to Adam.

As he began to talk about his brother Sam and the deep betrayal he'd felt at his brother's crime, Melanie ached for his pain and realized it had been far too long since she'd noticed somebody else's pain instead of her own.

"Sam harbored such bitterness because the person he thought was responsible for our sister's death had found happiness with a new woman, Lizzy Wiles," Adam explained. "Sam decided as long as he grieved for our sister, Daniel Jefferson needed to grieve, as well. Daniel's wife died in the car accident that Cherry died in. Rumor had it that Daniel's wife had called Cherry to pick her up after she and Daniel fought. In Sam's mind, everything became Daniel's fault, but nobody ever dreamed he'd actually try to hurt Lizzy." Adam shook his head. "It's a terrible thing, what that kind of bitterness can do to a person."

"Is there a possibility he'll get out of jail?"

"I don't know. He's got the best criminal defense lawyer that money can buy, but he needs to pay for what he tried to do and he needs some kind of mental help. It's like he snapped and went crazy. He's still not in touch with reality and hasn't taken responsibility for what he's done."

He looked so sad, she wanted to reach across the table and take his hand in hers, somehow console him with a physical touch. But she fought the impulse. She didn't want to feel anything for Adam except a nice friendship for the man who was renting her upstairs, and she was afraid that with a simple touch she'd want more and that would be the height of foolishness.

They lingered over coffee and the conversation turned to the murders that had rocked the town in recent months. "Tilly sees a serial killer in every shadow," she said with a touch of humor.

"A lot of women are jumping at shadows right now," Adam replied. "The sheriff and his men have been chasing their tails on these cases. Two women found dead in their beds and no evidence left behind."

"I can't believe that Jimmy Collins is now a deputy. He was kind of a skinny nerd in high school."

"He's not nerdy anymore. I'd say he's one of the most eligible bachelors in town."

"Next to you," she teased.

He released a rueful laugh. "Yeah, well, at the moment I'm nobody's prize. I'm just an out-of-work, non-drinking man renting the upstairs of a house from a lovely lady."

She knew he was so much more than that, but she realized if she wasn't careful, she'd develop some sort of hero worship thing where he was concerned. After all, he'd built her a ramp. He'd forced her to get out of the house. He was changing her life and probably didn't even know it.

Whatever he was going through in his own life was temporary. She figured within two or three months he'd be ready to move on and he'd start reaching for dreams that would never, could never include her.

They could be friends, but she had to remember that she would always just be his landlady. And after he left, hopefully there would be another boarder…and another and she'd live her life vicariously through the people who rented her upstairs.

"I don't know what you're thinking about, but I wish you would stop." Adam's voice pulled her from her reverie.

She looked at him in surprise. "Why? Was I making faces?"

"Just one face…a sad one. I absolutely don't allow a sad face at the dinner table!" he exclaimed with a ring of mock authority.

His teasing chased away her dismal thoughts.

"My sister, Cherry, used to say that we all make a choice each morning. We choose to either be happy or be sad. She was the happiest person I ever knew," he said with a touch of wistfulness.

"You miss her," Melanie said softly.

"Every day. And I'm sure you miss your mother."

Melanie took a sip of her coffee and leaned back in her chair. "I had a lot of time to prepare myself for Mom's passing. She was sick for a long time, but yes, I miss her."

"And what about your father?"

"He checked out of our lives when I was two. I wouldn't know him if he walked right up to me and said hello."

"He doesn't know what he missed out on," Adam replied.

She smiled and suddenly she'd had enough. She felt slightly overwhelmed by the clatter of dishes, the chatter of people and Adam's kindness.

By the time they left the café, twilight had fallen, deepening shadows beneath the trees and around buildings. Adam offered to push her and she relented and allowed him to do so.

"I should be wheeling myself to work off some of that chicken fried steak and potatoes," she said as she leaned back in the chair and relaxed. "But, to be perfectly honest, I'm completely exhausted."

She was aware that it was more of a mental exhaustion than a physical one. Her mouth ached from all the smiling she'd done and after months of near isolation she felt overstimulated and edgy.

"You did really well for your first time out."

She thought she felt his breath on the back of her neck, a provocative warmth that was oddly soothing. "It was nice to be out," she admitted.

"You have more friends than you think you have, Melanie. I wouldn't be surprised if your phone starts ringing off the hook with all kinds of invitations."

"I'm not ready to become a social butterfly just yet. Tonight was nice, but I want to take it all slow. I'm still adjusting to this darned chair and all the limitations in my life."

"The only limitations you have are those you put in your own mind."

She bit her bottom lip to keep from snapping at him. Easy for him to say. He was walking on his two feet. He could run after a toddler who was chasing a ball. He could dance a two-step. There were so many things he could do that she would never do again.

She was grateful when they reached her front door.

All she wanted now was the privacy of her own room. Adam unlocked the door and turned to look at her, and in the purple glow of evening she thought she saw a whisper of something inviting in his eyes. It was a look that said he wouldn't mind a kiss and she caught her breath as he half bent down toward her.

For just a minute she felt like a young woman coming home from a date, her chest filled with the anticipation of a first sweet kiss, a promise of something more to come.

She quickly backed up. She didn't want him to kiss her, because she realized she wanted him to kiss her. She wondered what his mouth would taste like, how his lips might play on her own. It would be the height of stupidity to allow a kiss to take place between them.

"Thanks, Adam," she said, surprised to find her voice lower, deeper than usual. "You can go on upstairs and I'll lock up from here."

He snapped straight up and stepped back from her. "Then I'll just say good-night," he said. With a nod of his head he turned and disappeared into the house.

Melanie pushed herself over the threshold, then turned her wheelchair around to close the front door. For just a moment she remained with the door open, drawing in deep breaths of the cool, autumn-scented night air.

All in all the outing had been a huge success. She'd been surprised to discover that Jim Collins was a deputy and Denver Walton was a mechanic and had been dating Maddy Billings for a long time. She'd dated both men briefly in high school, but she hadn't gotten serious about anyone. Dance had always taken precedence over boys and dating.

Even when she was living in New York City, there had been little time for dating. Life had pretty much revolved around auditions, rehearsals and performances. Most of the time a bunch of the cast of a particular show went out in a group to grab a bite to eat or have a few drinks or just unwind after a performance.

She'd had a relationship with a male dancer for three months, but different schedules and locations had eventually ended things between them.

Melanie hadn't been in love with him, nor had he been in love with her. Still, it had been nice for a while to have somebody to talk to, somebody to make her feel desirable, not just as a fellow dancer but as a woman. He'd taken away some of the loneliness that often set in when the stage lights went out for the night.

She started to close the door but paused as a movement just behind the big tree in the front yard caught her eye. She tightened her grip on the doorknob. Was there somebody there? Was somebody hiding?

"Hello?" she called softly.

Darkness had quickly usurped the last gasp of day and a sudden shiver raced down her spine. The person who had killed two waitresses who worked at the Cowboy Café could possibly still be roaming the streets.

Was it possible he'd changed his victim profile and now had her in his sights? She narrowed her eyes, trying to see what or who had moved and caught her gaze.

Nothing.

She slammed the door closed and carefully locked it.

Silly, she thought as she wheeled herself into her bedroom. It must have been all the talk about the murders that had prompted the faint whisper of fear that pumped her heart a little too fast.

She was no better than silly Tilly, seeing bogeymen in shadows. She'd obviously mistaken a swaying branch or a cat for something more ominous. Still, as she got into bed, she realized that the wind hadn't been blowing and the figure she'd thought she saw was far too big to be a cat.

Chapter 5

He'd wanted to kiss her. He'd wanted to kiss her so badly, it had ached in his bones an hour later, when he got into bed. And when he woke up the next morning, he still wanted to kiss her.

Adam pulled himself out of bed before dawn. He showered and dressed and then left the house, deciding to head to the ranch and take a sunrise horseback ride.

He had enjoyed his time with Melanie too much, had almost crossed the line she'd drawn in the sand when he moved in. Tenant and landlord, that was the only relationship she wanted with him, and if he screwed that up, he'd be out of a place to live and he wouldn't get a chance to spend more time with her.

The sun was just beginning to peek over the horizon as he reached the ranch. He went directly to the stables and saddled up his favorite mount, Jasper, and took off across the pasture.

He was attracted to Melanie like he'd never been attracted to a woman. He searched inside his heart, wondering if his fascination with her was simply pity for a woman whose life course had been halted abruptly by tragedy.

But no matter how hard he looked, he couldn't find pity there. When he'd gazed at the photos on the living room wall, he'd admired the talented woman she'd been, but he was far more intrigued by the woman she was now, the woman she would become as she sought a new way of living.

In the weeks and months ahead he looked forward to seeing how much character she had, if she had the strength to truly rise above what had happened to her. He hoped so; he wanted that for her.

He rode at a sedate gait for about a half an hour, his mind replaying the night out with Melanie. Finally he turned around to go back to the stables. He gave Jasper more rein and the horse responded by breaking into a brisk run.

The cool morning air emptied his head of all thoughts as he simply enjoyed the scent of pasture and autumn that rode a slight breeze.

The Benson ranch was very profitable and belonged to Sam, Adam and Nick. The profits were split between the three, providing a very good living for all of them. At the moment Sam's money was tied up in his defense, and Adam had insisted Nick take a bigger cut as he was the one taking care of the ranch now. Still, it provided a good lifestyle for Adam, although he'd always been rather frugal with his money. Without a wife or family, without even a girlfriend, there had been few things to spend his money on, so most of it had been put into savings.

When he reached the stables, Adam dismounted and gave Jasper a quick rubdown. He headed for the house in the distance, not ready to go back into town yet.

By this time he knew his brother's family would all be awake and hopefully Courtney would be in the middle of fixing some kind of breakfast.

The front door was unlocked, and he opened it and stepped into the foyer, which smelled of frying bacon and fresh-brewed coffee. "Anyone home?"

"Unc Dam!" Garrett came running toward him, diaper in hand. He was clad in a pajama top and nothing else.

"Hey, buddy. Aren't you supposed to be wearing that instead of carrying it?" Adam said with a grin.

Nick came chasing after Garrett, a look of frustration on his face. "He's the slipperiest worm on the planet." He scooped up the half-naked child. "Courtney's in the kitchen. Help yourself to the coffee, and I'll be in once I wrangle this little bull and get a diaper on him."

He disappeared down the hallway with a giggling Garrett as Adam headed for the kitchen. There were times when Adam envied his brother for finding love and for having a son. He admired the fact that Nick had never doubted his own sanity, had somehow managed to put Cherry's death and Sam's crime behind him to move forward to a happy place. Adam was still seeking his happy place.

As he entered the kitchen, Courtney turned to face him, a bright smile lighting her face. "I knew there was a reason that I decided to fry up some extra bacon this morning."

"Nothing like an unexpected guest for breakfast," Adam said as he walked over to the coffeemaker and poured himself a cup of the fragrant brew.

"Maybe unexpected, but never unwelcome," Courtney replied. "I heard you were out last night with your landlady." She began cracking eggs into a large mixing bowl.

"Wow. News travels fast." He sat down at the table and took a sip of his coffee.

"I heard it from a friend who heard it from a friend who said the two of you were eating dinner together at the café." She flashed him a wry grin. "So was it a date?"

"No," he replied hurriedly. "It was just an outing. I built a ramp from her front door to the sidewalk and this was her first trip out since she went into the wheelchair seven months ago."

Courtney turned to the skillet and flipped over several slices of bacon. "How did she do?"

"She was a little nervous, but she did just fine." Adam took a second sip of his coffee and thought about the night before. "I think it was a bit overwhelming for her and she was pretty exhausted by the time I took her home."

Once again he thought of that moment when they'd

been on her porch, when he'd wanted nothing more than to taste her lips. She'd just looked so darned kissable.

It was crazy. He'd known her for less than a week but he already somehow felt invested in her, in her life. He told himself his desire to kiss her had been nothing more than some strange phenomenon brought on by the moonlight and the way her blue blouse made her eyes appear so soulful and her lips look soft and yielding.

It had just been a wild moment, probably never to be repeated, he thought. In any case she had dismissed him quickly, as if she'd sensed what he was thinking and wanted no part of it.

"Adam?"

Courtney's voice penetrated his thoughts and he looked at her.

"I asked you if you wanted one piece of toast or two."

"One is fine," he replied.

Within minutes Nick and a fully dressed Garrett entered the room and breakfast was served. The food was great and the conversation was pleasant, with Garrett offering comic relief with his childish antics.

"I was planning on driving to Oklahoma City this morning to see a man who has a champion bull for sale. Want to take the ride with me?" Nick asked Adam.

It was a two-hour drive into the city, but Adam certainly had no other plans for the day. "Sure. It's a nice day for a drive."

"And I'd like the company," Nick replied.

An hour later, Adam and Nick were in Nick's truck and headed down the highway. Nick and Adam had never been particularly close. Adam had spent most of his time growing up in Sam's company, while Nick and Cherry had bonded together as the youngest siblings.

Cherry's death in the car accident had sent them all reeling, but Sam's arrest had nearly destroyed both of the brothers who remained behind to pick up the pieces. Nick had dealt with it by leaving town and going to Texas to work on a friend's ranch. And Adam, well, there had been those bottles of booze to ease his pain.

"So are you finding what you are looking for living in town?" Nick asked as he rolled down his window to let in the cool autumn air.

"I'm not sure exactly what I'm looking for," Adam replied honestly.

"You know there's always a place for you at the ranch."

"I know that, and I appreciate it, but it's just not where I want to be right now. I'm thinking about talking to Cameron about training or whatever I'd need to do to maybe become a deputy."

Nick shot him a look of surprise, which quickly faded and turned into a grin. "You always did like watching all those cop shows on TV and trying to solve the crime before the TV cops did. I imagine Cameron could use more help." He hesitated a moment and then continued, "Does this have something to do with Sam?"

It was Adam's turn to look at his brother in surprise. "What do you mean?"

"Oh, you know, you feel guilty about what he did and so you're going into law enforcement to ease some of that guilt and prove to the town that at least you're a good guy."

Adam considered his brother's words and then shook his head negatively. "Nah, you're looking way too deep. It's just something that's always been in the back of my mind, even before Sam was arrested. The ranch had started to feel like a ball and chain. I never loved it like you and Sam did. I just felt the weight of responsibility of doing a job I didn't really love."

"It's important to find your passion. Ranching has always been what I wanted to do, and reconnecting with Courtney was a gift. Between those two and Garrett, I've found a real passion for living each day."

"And I envy you that," Adam admitted.

Nick flashed him a quick grin. "You become a deputy and you'll have to fight off half the women in town. You know women love men in uniform."

Adam laughed and that seemed to set the tone for the remainder of the afternoon. Adam had forgotten how much he enjoyed his little brother's company, how humorous Nick could be, how easy he was to be around.

The drive to Oklahoma City seemed to fly by as the two talked about everything from their childhood to Cherry's death and to Sam's arrest.

"Have you talked to him lately?" Adam asked.

"Last week. His trial has been set for next month. Have you talked to him?"

Adam shook his head. "Not since the night he was arrested. I can't. I'm still so angry at him." He reached up and swiped a hand through his hair. Thoughts of Sam always made him feel slightly anxious.

"He's sick, Adam. Maybe it was the stress of him taking care of all of us for so long after Mom and Dad died, but Cherry's death drove him to a dark place with a sickness that simmered inside him for a long time."

"Yeah, I know. But we were so close. I should have sensed that something was off with him," Adam protested.

"You have to stop blaming yourself for not seeing it, for not sensing it. Sam alone is responsible for his actions, but it wouldn't hurt for him to know that you still care about him. He asks about you each time I talk to him."

Adam's heart squeezed tight. He'd loved Sam, at least the man Sam had been before he tried to kill somebody. "I'm just not ready to talk to him yet," he finally replied. "He calls occasionally but I don't accept the charges."

By that time they had reached the ranch where the bull was for sale. The ranch looked forlorn, with a barn that threatened to bite the dust beneath a light breeze and stock that was small and underfed.

Earl Waylan talked up his animals with an arrogance that bordered on obnoxious. The bull was small and timid and nothing that Nick was interested in buying.

"That bull looked like he'd run in the opposite direction if he saw a heifer," Nick said when they were back in the truck. He cast Adam a wry grin. "Kind of reminded me of you."

Adam laughed. "I'm not timid of heifers. It's women who freak me out just a little bit."

Nick grinned. "What about Melanie Brooks? Does she freak you out just a little bit?"

A vision of Melanie filled Adam's head. Melanie,

with her angel blond hair and haunting blue eyes, with her occasional sharp tongue and whisper of vulnerability. She definitely touched him.

"A little bit," Adam finally replied. "Although definitely in a good way."

"This isn't some desire of yours to help a helpless woman?" Nick asked.

"Melanie definitely isn't some poor, helpless woman. She takes care of herself just fine. She's intelligent and beautiful and I've got to admit there's something about her that draws me in."

"I thought you were the confirmed bachelor of Grady Gulch."

"I am," Adam replied firmly. "But that doesn't mean I can't enjoy the company of an attractive woman."

"Just don't break her heart," Nick warned. "I would imagine she's pretty vulnerable and you wouldn't want her to get the wrong idea."

"Don't worry. I'm sure we're both on the same page, just looking for a little companionship, that's all."

The day turned into evening and Adam stayed and ate dinner with his brother and his family. By the time he left the ranch, the purple dusk was beginning to fade into night.

Whenever he spent time with Nick and Courtney, he wondered what it would be like to be in love, to share those special glances with a woman, to know each other so well that you could read each other's minds, finish each other's sentences.

He didn't trust himself to have that kind of relationship and yet there were moments of silence in his life that he wished were filled by another's voice, when he longed to have somebody who cared for him, somebody he could love more than anyone else on the face of the earth.

But he'd loved his parents and they had died. He'd loved his sister, Cherry, and she was gone, as well. He'd looked up to Sam and he had betrayed him. Was it any wonder that Adam was a bit gun-shy when it came to putting his heart on the line?

By the time he parked his truck in Melanie's driveway, it was almost nine. Her usual habit was to retire to her room around eight-thirty or so.

He opened the door and came in quietly. As he entered the living room, his gaze automatically went in the direction of Melanie's bedroom.

He froze. Her bedroom door was halfway open, allowing him a view of the bottom half of her bed. He could also see the bottom of her midnight blue nightgown and her slender bare legs beneath. She was sitting up and appeared to be rubbing the calf of her right leg.

He hadn't ever considered that she might have actual pain. He'd just assumed that her leg was numb... dead. But as he stepped closer, he could hear her emitting soft, whispery moans as her hands worked up and down her leg.

Without realizing what he was doing, he moved to her doorway. She looked up, her eyes widening, obviously startled by his presence.

He didn't speak; he wasn't sure if he could if he wanted to. Instead he walked over to the foot of the bed and sat down, then pulled her leg into his lap, surprised when she didn't fight him.

He began to massage it like she had done, up and down her calf with just a light pressure. Her feet were bare, her toenails painted a pearly pink. Her right foot pointed downward in an unnatural resting position. A perfect ballerina point for a ballerina who couldn't dance, he thought.

"Can you stand on it at all?" he asked.

"I can stand on my left foot and balance a bit with the right but not for long," she replied. "The right foot and leg really have no function at all."

"Does it hurt often?" He hated the idea of her being in pain.

"From the knee down it's a chronic ache with electric tingles and what I call zingers. It's hard to explain the pain. It's usually manageable, but sometimes, like tonight, it becomes a bit unbearable."

"Do you have medicine to take?" he asked, half mesmerized by her skin beneath his hands. It was like stroking fine silk.

"I have pain pills, but I never take them during the day and only occasionally at night. I don't like feeling drugged up and the pills don't really take away all the pain."

"But if it hurts, you should at least get a little relief and take a pill." He wasn't looking at her, but rather his gaze was captured by the sight of his big, bronzed hands against her pale, slender leg. She had dancer's legs, slim, but with calf muscles that gave them shape.

Her scent filled the room, clean and floral and utterly captivating. He closed his eyes for a long moment, just breathing in her essence.

When he did look at her again, her eyes were dark pools of midnight blue and her lower lip looked full and inviting. Once again his need to kiss her hit him full force in the pit of his stomach, nearly stealing the breath from his body.

She appeared to be holding her breath and her nipples were erect against the silk material of her nightgown. Adam's blood heated in his body and he realized he was fully aroused.

There was a part of him that was half confused by the effect she had on him, by the physical attraction that was a visceral force inside him. All he'd meant to do was alleviate some of her pain, but somehow touching her had completely turned him on. There was also a part of him that recognized that she appeared to be affected in the same way.

It's easier to beg for forgiveness than ask for permission. The same words he'd thought as he'd built her ramp now screamed inside his head.

He stopped manipulating her calf and in a swift, fluid movement slid closer to her, close enough that he leaned forward and pressed his lips to hers.

She stiffened. He mentally winced, believing he'd misread the signals, misread her and that he definitely would need to beg for forgiveness, but before he could pull away, her lips softened and opened to him.

He fell into the soft, sweet taste of her mouth, swirling his tongue with hers as all other thoughts were driven from his head.

She responded by leaning forward slightly as the kiss grew deeper. She tasted just as he'd imagined she would, like sweet fire that ignited a flame in the pit of his stomach.

It wasn't until he began to wrap his arms around her that she once again stiffened and drew back from him. He instantly slid backward and got off the bed. Her lips were red; her eyes glazed with a hazy light.

Adam raked a hand through his hair and offered her a tight smile. "I'd apologize for that, but to be perfectly honest I'm not a bit sorry."

The haze in her eyes slowly faded and she sat up straighter against the pillows behind her back. "And I'd demand an apology if I hadn't wanted you to do that. But now that it's been done, we both need to forget it occurred and make sure it doesn't happen again."

She picked up a prescription bottle from the table next to her bed. "I think I will take that tonight. I'll see you in the morning."

It was an obvious dismissal. Adam hesitated a moment, wanting to say something, but in the end he nodded and left her room. What he wanted to do was ask her why on earth it couldn't happen again.

Chapter 6

The memory of that unexpected kiss filled Melanie's head for the next three days. Adam's mouth had been hot...hungry against hers and she'd wanted to lose herself in his heat, but she'd stopped the kiss before things had spiraled out of control.

And it would have been so easy for her to allow the escalation of the kiss, but she didn't trust it. Although she'd appreciated his gentleness in massaging her leg, she didn't trust him. What man in his right mind would want to start something with a woman like her?

She was no fool. Adam Benson was just passing time here in her house and with her. He was a cowboy boarder and nothing else. She'd gladly take his rent money, but she couldn't allow him to get into her heart in any meaningful way, because she knew with a certainty that she would never be in his heart.

Sure, he might want to kiss her, he might even want to take things further, but he was in transition, unsure of where he belonged in life, within himself. The one thing she knew to be true was that he didn't belong here with her.

Since the kiss, he had gotten up early in the morning and had stayed away from the house, arriving back only at night to go upstairs. When they did happen to be in the same room at the same time, there was a painful politeness between them that made her want to scream.

She now glanced at the clock in the kitchen. Two o'clock. A glance out the window made her bones chill. It was a blustery day, the wind blowing with a briskness that portended the winter still to come.

A nice hot cup of tea. Maybe that would banish the chill that threatened to overtake her when she thought of winter, when she thought of Adam.

He stirred something in her, something that had never been stirred before. He made her think of all the things she hadn't thought of before...like loving and marriage and children.

There hadn't been time for those kinds of thoughts, those kinds of yearnings when she was a working dancer. She'd always assumed eventually she'd have all that, once her career was winding down. It was only since she'd met Adam that a strange, alien wistfulness had welled up inside her, a vague desire for something more in her life, something more than what she had now, something more than being a dancer.

She wheeled over to the cabinet where she kept the teakettle and opened the door, surprised to see an empty shelf where the teakettle should be.

Had she mindlessly placed it in another one of the lower cabinets? She went down the line, checking in each one, but there was no teakettle to be found.

With a frown she eyed the upper cabinets. Had Adam used it and put it in one of them? An irrational irritation filled her. Didn't he realize it was difficult for her to get to those upper cabinets? Had that kiss somehow made him forget that she was a cripple?

For one fleeting moment she wondered if he'd done it on purpose, to somehow punish her for halting what he'd begun in her bedroom two nights before.

She instantly dismissed the unkind thought. She knew instinctively that Adam wasn't the kind of man to play wicked games. Still, when she finally balanced carefully on her good foot and rose up enough to check the upper cabinet, she found the teakettle there. She told herself that she needed to remind him that if he used something from the lower cabinets, he better put it back where it belonged.

The tea didn't help. It didn't warm her nor did it take away any of the edgy tension that had been her constant companion for the last couple of days.

She nearly jumped out of her chair at the unusual sound of the phone ringing. She quickly wheeled over to the phone on the counter and checked the caller ID. She didn't recognize the number but answered, anyway. "Hello?"

She waited for a response but none was forthcoming. "Hello?" she said again. She knew somebody was on the line. She could hear the sound of deep, uneven breathing.

"Who is this? Craig, is this you?" A wave of anger swept over her as she thought of the real estate man. But as the sound of breathing continued and no words were spoken, an inexplicable fear raced through her and she slammed down the receiver.

She nibbled on her bottom lip, staring at the phone. Surely if it had been Craig, he would have said something. So who had been on the phone?

Maybe it had been some weird cell phone disconnect or a telemarketer who had gotten interrupted. Still, it bothered her enough that she grabbed a pen and paper and punched the caller ID button to display the number the call had originated from. She scribbled it down and then tried to call it back, unsurprised when she got an automated response that the cell phone caller was unavailable at the moment and to try again later.

The whole incident simply fed the edginess that had been with her for the past couple of days. She suddenly found the silence around her oppressive.

She had apparently gotten too used to having Adam around and was feeling the isolation of the last three days of him being gone most of the time.

It was the first time since she'd gone into the wheelchair that she wanted out of the house, to be among other people. But she moved back to the kitchen table and stared into the backyard, remembering the night that she and Adam had gone to the café and she'd thought she'd seen somebody hiding behind the tree in her front yard.

She leaned back in her chair and rubbed a hand across her forehead. She'd slept unusually hard the night before, after taking one of her pain pills.

When she'd awakened, she'd been groggy, and only after a shower and dressing had she felt more like herself. She hadn't left the kitchen all day, but now, staring out the back window, she realized the view was starting to bore her.

Could she wheel herself to the café for dinner? Leave the house under her own steam and eat dinner among other people? A week ago she never would have considered it. Adam had opened up a little piece of the world for her in the week he'd been living here. She just wasn't sure she was in a place to explore it all alone.

Instead of leaving the house, she went into her bedroom and grabbed the sketch pad that had traveled with her for the past ten years. Inside were sketches of dance costumes, along with written choreography of the dances she'd seen in her mind as she'd drawn the costumes.

This was the one hobby she'd had aside from the actual dancing. She'd always known in the back of her mind that a day would come when she'd no longer be fresh and exciting, when she'd be deemed too old for the stage. She'd just assumed when that time came, she'd come back home and open a dance studio of her own, a place to feed the dreams of little girls.

Of course, she'd always assumed when that time came, she'd be in her thirties, still young enough to open a dance studio, maybe find love and build a family. She hadn't expected an injury in the best years of her dancing career, an injury that would keep her from teaching, from loving.

She was still sketching at the kitchen table when Adam entered the house close to five o'clock. Just the sight of him in his worn, tight jeans and long-sleeved navy polo shirt set off that crazy yearning inside her, a yearning she battled with a stir of anger.

"Did you use my teakettle this morning?" she asked as she closed the sketchbook in front of her.

He looked at her in surprise. "No. I don't drink hot tea. Why?"

"I found my teakettle in the upper cabinet and I thought maybe you'd used it and had forgotten to put it back where it belonged."

He held up both hands. "I swear, I'm innocent. Did you ask Tilly?"

"She hasn't been in today," Melanie replied.

He walked over to the refrigerator and pulled out a cold soda, and when he turned to face her, a touch of humor lit his eyes. "Ah, so what we have here is the case of the misplaced teakettle. What are your thoughts, Watson?"

Her mood lightened. "My thoughts are why do you get to be Sherlock and I just get to be your sidekick?"

He pretended to stroke a beard thoughtfully. "Because I'm the one thinking about a career in law enforcement. Besides, if I get a motorcycle, you can ride in my sidecar, thus making you my sidekick."

She gave a mock groan at his ridiculous rationale

and realized that she'd missed his company over the last couple of days. "Have you eaten?" she asked.

"No. What about you?" He remained leaning against the refrigerator door, looking so handsome he half stole her breath away.

"Not since lunch."

"How about I throw a couple of steaks under the broiler and you can make a salad?" he suggested.

"Sounds like a plan," she agreed.

For the next half an hour they bustled around the kitchen with an easy camaraderie, which chased away any earlier loneliness Melanie might have felt.

Adam was such fun. He made a big production of seasoning the steaks, as if he were a master chef. She found herself laughing over and over again at his antics.

Once the meal was ready, they sat across from each other at the table and talked about family and growing up in Grady Gulch.

"Growing up in Grady Gulch was like being in Mayberry," he said.

She nodded, knowing exactly what he was talking about. "There was an innocence, as if we were all invincible against the kind of crime and evil we heard about on the news. I remember leaving the house after dinner and not coming back until the lightning bugs started flickering, and I was never afraid."

"Everyone knew everyone else and I wouldn't have understood the concept of stranger danger." He cut into his thick, juicy steak.

"It's sad that the murders have destroyed an innocence that might have still been here," she replied.

"It's tragic," he agreed.

"And the sad part is that once that innocence has been shattered, you never really get it back." She sighed. "It would just be nice if Cameron could get the bad guy off the streets for good."

"Maybe he needs Sherlock on his team," Adam said teasingly.

"With his sidekick, Watson," she added.

Their lighthearted conversation continued as they cleaned up the kitchen and then moved to the living room.

It was just after nine when she called it a night. Not so much because she was tired, but rather because she realized she was enjoying his company far too much.

She hadn't forgotten how his mouth had felt over hers, and the longer she spent with him, the more she wanted him to kiss her again. Definitely time to call an end to the night when those kinds of thoughts refused to get out of her head.

"Thanks for the great steak," she said as they made their way to the foot of the stairs.

"Thanks for the great company," he replied, his gaze far too warm as it lingered on her.

"Good night, Adam," she said firmly and wheeled backward in an effort to circumvent anything else that might happen.

"Sweet dreams, Melanie," he replied.

She watched as he climbed the stairs, and then turned and went into her bedroom to prepare for bed. There was something about shared laughter that created a special kind of intimacy between two people.

They shared the same sense of humor and she found that sexy as heck. He got her and she got him. But it could never be anything more than what it was.

She had to stop thinking about his kiss, quit fantasizing about how his big, strong hands might feel touching not just her leg, but her entire body.

She wheeled herself into the bathroom. *Foolish thoughts from a foolish mind,* she told herself. It took her only minutes to scrub her face and brush her teeth. Then she whirled her wheelchair around to reach for the nightgown and robe that she always kept on a hook on the back of her bathroom door. Neither were there.

She frowned at the empty hook. What was going on? Part of the way she functioned independently was by being a creature of habit, by having a place for everything and everything in its place.

So where were her robe and nightgown? She gazed around the bathroom in stunned disbelief. Tilly hadn't been in to take them off the hook for laundering. Just like she hadn't been there that day to move the teakettle, Melanie reminded herself.

She wheeled herself out of the bathroom and back into her bedroom, feeling as if she was losing her mind. She *always* hung her night things on that hook. So why weren't they there?

She spied her nightgown, a blue puddle on the floor, next to the chair that sat by the window. She wheeled over and picked it up. A few minutes later she found her robe hanging on a hanger in her clothes closet.

Returning the robe to the hook in the bathroom, she wondered if she was going crazy. Had she tossed her nightgown toward the chair that morning, when she'd dressed? She certainly didn't remember doing it, just like she didn't remember hanging her robe up in the closet.

But nobody else had been in her bedroom all day. She must have done it. As she climbed into bed, her heart beat an unsteady rhythm.

Was it possible that the malfunction in her leg had more far-reaching consequences than she'd initially thought? Was it possible that the neuropathy wasn't just in her leg but was somehow worming its way into her brain? It was a frightening thought that kept her awake deep into the night.

Adam awakened the next morning with the decision to go ahead and put the railings up on the ramp he'd built. The railings would make the ramp safer for Melanie if she decided to use it alone and he was encouraged by the fact that she'd already used it once to go to the Cowboy Café with him.

The night before had been magical. Melanie had appeared more relaxed than he'd ever seen her and he'd loved the sound of her laughter as the evening progressed.

As he showered, he tried to focus on the task ahead rather than think about her. He didn't want to overanalyze things. Last night she'd been open and fun, but he also knew that she could just as easily go back to isolating herself.

One day at a time, he told himself as he got dressed for the day. Although he recognized that his feelings for her deepened each minute they spent together, he also recognized that ultimately he was her tenant, not her boyfriend.

He was vaguely disappointed when he went down to the kitchen and found that the coffee had been made but there was no sign of Melanie and her bedroom door was closed.

Maybe she'd made the coffee and then returned to her room to get dressed for the day. He poured himself a cup and carried it to the table and sat, his mind working to make a mental list of the supplies he'd need to buy for the railings on the ramp.

By the time he'd finished his second cup of coffee, he realized Melanie didn't appear to be inclined to make a morning appearance. He rinsed out his cup and placed it in the dishwasher, then grabbed his hat and headed out the front door.

The early morning sun was unusually warm on his shoulders as he headed to his truck. It was going to be a perfect day to do a little carpentry work outside.

He couldn't help that his thoughts went back to Melanie as he drove to the lumber store. Last night it had felt so right, cooking with her, eating across from her and then later talking and laughing together.

He felt as if he were walking a tightrope where she was concerned. He didn't want to screw up his living arrangement but he also wasn't satisfied just being her tenant.

He had to allow her to take the lead, and for the first time in his life Adam wished he were the one in control, wished he held all the cards in what might come next between him and his lovely landlady.

He parked in the lumber store parking lot and got out of the truck, eager to get the required materials and get started on his task.

As he headed inside, he saw Thomas Manning just ahead of him. "Tom," he shouted in greeting.

The tall, thin man turned around and offered Adam a pleasant smile. "Hi, Adam."

"Got a project planned?" Adam asked as the two went through the front door of the store together. He looked at Thomas curiously. Although he was pleasant enough, he stayed to himself, even when dining at the café.

"Not a project. Just some handyman things that need to be taken care of around the house," Thomas replied. "What about you?"

"Have a little outdoor project to complete and figured I'd better get it done before the weather turns," Adam replied.

"Definitely nice weather for anything outside," Thomas agreed.

The men parted ways as Thomas headed for the hardware section of the store and Adam went toward the lumber. As he picked up the items he'd need to build the railings, his thoughts lingered on Thomas.

Adam had never heard much about the man. Nobody seemed to know what he did for a living, and he was rarely seen outside his house unless he was dining at the Cowboy Café. He lived alone and seemed to like it that way.

He wondered if Cameron had thoroughly checked out his background. The murders of the two waitresses hadn't occurred until after Thomas had moved to town.

He frowned and told himself he was certain that Cameron was on top of things and everyone in the entire town had come under close scrutiny after the murders.

It was almost ten by the time he got back to Melanie's. He'd just started unloading the lumber when Kevin Naperson came walking toward him.

"Whatever you're doing, I'd be glad to help for a little cash," Kevin said.

Adam's first instinct was to tell the kid no, that he didn't need any help. But Kevin looked so eager and Adam knew he'd had a tough time since the death of his girlfriend, Candy, especially since he'd initially been Cameron's number one suspect in the murder.

"Never mind," Kevin said, as if he could feel Adam's hesitation. "I guess if I'm going to find work, I'm going to have to leave town." He started to walk past, but Adam stopped him.

He offered the kid a fair wage for helping with the railings and together they got to work.

"Life been tough?" Adam asked as they unloaded the lumber from the back of the truck.

"You have no idea," Kevin replied. "I mean, at first I understood why I was a suspect in Candy's murder. I was her boyfriend, we'd had a fight at the Corral that night and I was the last person to see her alive. But everyone forgot somehow that she was my girlfriend, that I was crazy about her, and I didn't even get a chance to feel bad about her death before everyone came at me, believing I killed her."

"And you didn't." Adam made it more of a statement than a question.

"Candy and I had our issues, but I loved her. I would have never hurt her, but half the people in this town still look at me like I'm some crazed madman."

Adam remembered how he had felt in the weeks following Sam's arrest, as if everyone was staring at him, as if he was responsible for Sam's actions.

Cameron had never been able to tie Kevin to either Candy's murder or Shirley's and there was something in the young man's eyes that made Adam believe he was innocent.

It took nearly two hours to get the railings up, and during that time the more Adam talked with Kevin, the more convinced he was that he was yet another victim of the killer. Kevin was virtually an outcast in his hometown just because he'd fallen in love with a young woman who'd been murdered.

Finished with the job, Adam went inside to get some lunch. He found Melanie seated at the table.

"I saw that you put up the railings on the ramp," she said in greeting. "I don't know how I'm ever going to thank you for everything you've done."

"No thanks necessary," he replied. It took him only a minute to read her mood. Withdrawn, distracted. He sank down in a chair across the table from her. "Everything okay?"

"Fine," she replied, although neither the tone of

her voice nor the shadows in her eyes convinced him. "Wasn't that Kevin Naperson out there helping you?"

"Yeah. I kind of feel sorry for the kid. He seems kind of lost and he told me he feels like everyone in town has turned their backs on him."

"From what you told me, he was a major suspect in the murders. What's your gut instinct about him, Sherlock?" Although she said the words teasingly, the shadows in her eyes didn't lift.

"Actually, my gut instinct is that he didn't have anything to do with the murders, but for all I know, he pulls the legs off puppy dogs in his spare time and is a sadistic killer."

"That's a cheerful thought," she replied dryly.

"Speaking of cheerful, you don't look so happy today."

She leaned back in her chair and raked a hand through her hair. "I guess I'm battling a little absent-mindedness. The teakettle wasn't where it belonged again this morning, and it took me forever to find my favorite tea, which is usually right next to the kettle. I finally found the tea bags in the refrigerator." She shrugged and gave him a rueful smile. "A mind is a terrible thing to lose."

"Don't worry about it. I'm sure it's just a temporary thing." He fought the impulse to lean across the table, to cover her hand with his. There was something about her posture, about the set of her shoulders that warned him to do so would be a mistake.

It wasn't until much later that night that Adam realized that talking to Kevin, letting the young man work on the railings with him might have been a mistake.

If Kevin was the person who had killed two help-less women in Grady Gulch, then by allowing him to help with the ramp, Adam had drawn his attention to the fact that inside the house was another woman who might be an easy target.

Chapter 7

Melanie awakened slightly cranky and more than a little bit groggy the next morning. She'd had a bad night with her leg. The pain had been unrelenting and she'd finally broken down and taken not only one, but two of the pain pills to gain some relief.

What she had gotten was some easing of the pain in exchange for horrible nightmares. She'd dreamed of slashing knifes and being chased down a dark street in her wheelchair. But the most disturbing had been her dreams of dancing puppets with broken legs and ballerinas leaping off cliffs.

The morning sun had been a welcome sight and after a long, hot shower some of the grogginess had been sloughed away. She'd dressed and gone straight into the kitchen, where gratefully she found her teakettle and tea just where they were supposed to be.

As she sat at the table and enjoyed a hot cup of the plum-flavored tea, which was her favorite, she thought about the crazy events of the day before.

Maybe it was just a case of her being distracted. She hadn't been paying attention to where she was putting things. And her distraction had a name—Adam.

The man invaded her thoughts no matter what she was doing, making it difficult for her to concentrate on anything. She found herself alternating between wanting to run to him and to run away, seek out his company and isolate herself from him.

He had her topsy-turvy with warring emotions and she didn't seem to be able to gain control of them. She told herself she wanted nothing more than a friendly landlord-tenant relationship, but when his lips curved up in one of his sexy smiles, when his eyes took on that delightful twinkle, she wanted more.

Was it any wonder she was putting things in the wrong places and feeling like she was losing her mind? It was his fault for being so darned sexy.

She took a sip of her tea and stared out the window, grateful to have a few minutes alone before he made his morning appearance. He filled the room when he entered it, bringing with him that male vitality, that familiar scent that stirred her on a decidedly pleasant level.

Drat the man, anyway, she thought crossly. It would have been easier had he been a drunk with bad manners who had to be tossed out on his ear.

She glanced at the clock and realized it was after

nine. Adam was either sleeping really late or he had gotten up very early and had left the house. She wouldn't be surprised if he'd left. She knew he occasionally got up early and headed for the ranch to eat breakfast with his brother's family.

Tilly called to tell her that she wouldn't be over that day and Melanie assured her she'd be fine on her own. Grabbing her sketch pad from the bedroom, Melanie returned to the kitchen, deciding that a bit of drawing would keep her mind occupied.

She stopped at noon and made herself a peanut butter and jelly sandwich and then returned to her sketching, happy to lose herself in her own little world without thoughts of Adam or her absentmindedness to intrude.

The next time she looked up from her work was when she heard the door open and close and realized Adam must have returned home. She was stunned to realize it was almost five o'clock. She'd spent the entire day at the kitchen table.

"Hi," she greeted him as he entered the kitchen. "Did you have a good day?"

"Yeah, I went out to the ranch and helped Nick with some fencing that needed to be repaired." His eyes were dark, cautious. "How about you? How are you feeling?"

"Fine. Why?"

"I just wondered if maybe you were still in the midst of the temper tantrum you must have had last night, after I went to bed."

She looked at him in surprise. "Temper tantrum? What are you talking about?"

"The pictures in the living room." There was an edge of tension wafting off him.

"What about them?"

"The glass is broken in all of them. Didn't you see them?" He frowned at her.

"No, I haven't been in the living room today." And the truth was she consciously didn't look at the pictures of herself dancing whenever she was in that room. It hurt too much.

She now wheeled past him into the living room, and as she looked at the wall of photos, her breath caught painfully in her chest. The covering glass on each and every photo either had been broken, leaving the picture still intact, or had shattered and fallen to the floor. Some of the shards sparkled on the floor in the late afternoon sunshine drifting through the window.

She was aware of Adam standing at the threshold between the kitchen and the living room. "They were like this when I got up this morning," he said. "I just assumed you'd gotten angry or hit a depressive low or something and did it sometime in the middle of the night."

"I didn't do this," she said, although it was more of a question than a statement. She remembered her disturbing dreams of the night before.

"I certainly didn't do it," he replied with a hint of indignation in his tone.

"And you didn't use my teakettle and put it away in one of the upper cabinets?" she asked, her mind whirling with horrible suppositions.

"No."

She stared at the broken glass, her heart beating a frantic rhythm. Was it possible she'd gotten up in the middle of the night, slid into her wheelchair and come in here to destroy the pictures?

Was it possible she herself had placed the teakettle in the upper cabinet? That she'd hung her robe in the closet and thrown her nightgown on the chair? She certainly didn't remember doing any of those things, but that didn't mean she hadn't done them.

The idea that anyone else had somehow come into the house to break the pictures or hide her teakettle was ludicrous and she knew by the perplexed expression on Adam's face that he wasn't responsible for the mess.

That left only her. Had the pain pills addled her mind so much that she had attempted to destroy the physical evidence of who, of what she'd once been? Of who she would never be again?

Or maybe it hadn't been the pain pills at all. Maybe it really was true. Maybe the trauma that had taken away her ability to walk had also affected her brain. Maybe her self-hatred was more intense than she'd thought.

She wrapped her arms around her shoulders to stanch the chill that threatened to suffuse her. She'd written it all off to the fact that she'd been distracted, but now she had to face a new possibility.

Maybe she was going insane.

It was almost two hours later that Adam sat across from Melanie at the kitchen table. He'd cleaned up the glass mess in the living room while she'd fixed a pot of tomato soup and grilled cheese sandwiches for dinner.

They had spoken very little while they'd each gone about their separate tasks. He'd been concerned when he'd left that morning after seeing the glass all broken, but afraid of stepping over the line, especially since the kiss, he'd left without checking in on her. He'd reminded himself that what she did in her own home was really none of his business, but he'd definitely been unsettled by what he'd seen.

He had spent most of the morning helping out Nick and then had gone to the sheriff's office and talked to Cameron about what he needed to do to become a deputy for the town. He was surprised to learn that all he needed was to be over the age of twenty-one, have no criminal past and a valid driver's license.

He'd filled out an application, and Cameron had told him he'd put it on file as at the moment Cameron had a full force and no funds to hire any more deputies.

In the meantime he'd suggested that Adam take a few courses in criminal justice at the community college and spend as much time as possible at the firing range on the outskirts of town.

But as he now sat across from Melanie, the events of his own day were the last things on his mind. He wished he knew her well enough to read her mind, to know what words would take the darkness away from her eyes.

They ate in an awkward silence, the only sound the scrape of their spoons against their bowls as they ate the warm soup. He had so many questions about what had happened the night before. He finally couldn't stand it any longer. He set his spoon down and gazed at her.

"Talk to me, Melanie. You don't remember anything about breaking the pictures?"

She raised her eyes to look at him and in the simmering depths of them he saw fear. "The only thing I remember about last night was nightmares, horrible dreams about dying dancers." Her spoon clattered to the table as if her fingers didn't have the strength to hold it another moment.

She went on. "How could I have done that and not remembered? But it had to be me. I mean, that's the only thing that makes sense and yet it doesn't make any sense. Did you hear anything? Breaking glass?"

He shook his head. "No, but I'm sleeping in the bedroom farthest from the living room. I hear street noises more than I hear anything from down here."

She rubbed the center of her forehead, as if a headache threatened to blossom there. "First there was the teakettle, then my robe and nightgown and now this."

"What about your robe and nightgown?"

She quickly explained to him about how those articles of clothing hadn't been where they were supposed to be the night before. "Then there was that weird phone call where somebody was just breathing on the line. Maybe I just imagined that."

"That's easy enough to check." Adam got up from the table and grabbed the cordless phone and handed it to her. "Check the caller ID. Show me what phone call you're talking about. It should be easy, because you don't get that many calls."

She nodded and punched the button for the history of calls. There were several calls from Tilly, but no number that didn't belong there. "It's not here," she said flatly as she handed the phone back to Adam. "I must be going crazy." She rubbed her forehead once again.

"You aren't crazy," Adam scoffed. "You're under stress. Your leg has been bothering you. You have somebody living under your roof. You might be doing some strange things, but you definitely aren't crazy."

She flashed him a grateful smile. The gesture lasted only a moment and then her lips turned downward. "One thing is for certain. I'm never taking one of those pain pills again!" she exclaimed.

"You took one last night?"

"Two," she admitted. "My leg and foot were giving me fits, so I took one about ten and then around ten-thirty I took another one."

She wheeled back from the table and into the living room, where she carefully transferred herself from the chair to the sofa. Adam followed and sat next to her, wanting to somehow comfort her as tears began to fill her eyes.

"I feel like I've lost everything that meant anything to me and now I'm slowly losing my mind." As her tears began to trek down her cheeks, she lowered her head in obvious despair.

Aware that once again he was treading on dangerous ground, he pulled her into his arms. She remained stiff for a long moment and then collapsed against him as her tears became deep, wrenching sobs.

He held her without saying a word, knowing that anything he might say would only be salt on her wounds. To tell her she hadn't lost something important was a lie. To tell her to buck up and face what had happened to her was insensitive. He knew instinctively what she needed at the moment was his silent support and his arms around her.

Despite the fact that she was crying, he couldn't help but notice that he liked the feel of her slender body against him, that as he ran his hands down her arms, he could feel sinewy muscle that attested to the upper body strength she possessed.

She cried until she was all cried out and then she pulled herself to an upright position with a small embarrassed laugh. "I'm sorry," she said as she wiped the tears from her eyes.

"Don't apologize. You're upset."

"You're a nice man, Adam, but I'm sure you didn't move in here to be my crying towel. You can go on upstairs if you want. I'll be fine."

He frowned. "You aren't dismissing me so easily this time," he said and made no move away from her.

Her gaze left his and once again went to the wall of photos. "I've been so angry about everything. Maybe last night, with my pills and the crazy bad dreams, I finally vented that anger in an outward, physical way."

"And hopefully the outburst has allowed you to get rid of the anger and move into the acceptance phase of all this."

She chewed on her lower lip, a look of fear darkening her eyes. "I hope so." Tension rolled off her in waves.

She leaned her head back against the sofa, looking as lovely as he'd ever seen her despite the redness of her eyes. "The anger has felt safe for so long. It was easy and had become comfortable. I don't know how to feel about acceptance. I don't even know if I'll ever gain total acceptance."

He fought the impulse to stroke the shiny hair that splayed out from her head against the back of the chocolate-brown sofa. "Trust me, I know how difficult acceptance of life's curveballs can be."

She looked at him curiously. "What do you mean?"

"My brother Sam has been in jail, awaiting trial, for over three months. He calls me about once a week but I never take his calls." Tension twisted tight in his stomach. "I'm still so angry with him, with what he tried to do, that I'm just not ready to talk to him." He frowned. "I think there's a part of me that is afraid if I get too close to Sam, I might discover some of the same antisocial traits in myself."

"That's ridiculous," she replied. "You are the kindest man I know, Adam. You aren't capable of doing what Sam tried to do." She released a small laugh. "We're quite a pair."

"We're a pair that left the dinner dishes on the table." He knew if he sat here next to her another minute, he would want to hold her in his arms once again. He would want to kiss her.

"Why don't you sit tight and relax and I'll take care of the cleanup?" he said as he stood.

"I don't need help," she protested, although without the bite in her voice he'd come to expect when he tried to do things for her.

"I know, but it's not every day I offer to take care

of the dishes, so I suggest you take me up on the offer when it's made."

Once again she smiled at him and he wanted to capture that smile in his heart forever. "Okay. Knock yourself out."

As he returned to the kitchen, he frowned, wondering about the broken glass from the pictures and the misplaced teakettle. If she'd gotten a phone call, why hadn't it shown up on her caller ID? It was possible that Tilly had accidently moved the teakettle the day before, when she'd been in to clean, but there was no way the older woman would have moved Melanie's clothing or destroyed the photos of the woman she considered a daughter.

The only conclusion he could draw was that Melanie had done the damage herself in a drug-induced expression of whatever bad dreams and self-anger she'd suffered. He believed in his heart that the act of violence was an anomaly and obviously directed only at herself and what she had once been.

It didn't scare him. His heart broke for her. It was obvious she was drifting in a sea of confusion, unsure where she now fit in the world. Surely that was what was causing her to do things she didn't remember. He had to believe that, but if these kinds of things continued, he'd have to talk to her about seeing a doctor.

He hadn't seen warning signs of madness in Sam, but from now on he intended to keep a close eye on Melanie and make sure if she really needed help, she'd get it.

It took him only minutes to clear their dishes from

the table and put them into the dishwasher and then he returned to the living room, where she hadn't changed positions on the sofa.

He returned to his spot next to her and for a long moment silence prevailed. "I spoke to Cameron today about what I need to do to become a deputy."

"Good for you," she replied. "And what did he tell you?"

"That the qualifications for becoming a deputy here in Grady Gulch are darned few, but he has no funds to hire a new deputy at this time."

"What will you do if a position doesn't open up here?"

He shrugged. "Look at some of the other small towns in the area and see if I can get hired on."

"You wouldn't feel bad about leaving Grady Gulch?" she asked.

He hesitated a long moment before replying. "Sure I would. This is my home and I love it here. I love the people here. I can't imagine a week going by that I'm not eating at the Cowboy Café, interacting with friends and neighbors. But if at some point I have to accept that there isn't a job here, then I'll have to move on."

"There's that *accept* word again," she said ruefully and he laughed. She frowned. "At least you have a plan."

He gazed at her curiously. "You never considered that a time might come when you would no longer be able to perform?"

"You know the old saying. Those who can do and those who can't teach. I'd just assumed when the time came that I was no longer viable as a performer, then I'd open a dance school here in Grady Gulch. Other than that I hadn't made any alternative life plans."

A frown danced across her forehead once again. "But let's not talk about this anymore. Tell me about happy times, Adam. Talk to me about your family when you were all young. Talk to me about Christmases past and Fourth of July celebrations."

And that was exactly what he did.

He spoke of birthday parties and town festivals. They laughed together as he told her about searching the house for Christmas presents and crying when he found them, because he knew he'd ruined his own surprise on Christmas morning.

Many of the stories revolved around Adam and Sam, and as he told her the funny things that had happened with the two of them he felt a yearning for all that had been lost and would never be again.

"Now, tell me some things about your childhood here in Grady Gulch. Surely you have some nice memories," he said.

"I do," she agreed. "As you know, it was a wonderful place to grow up. Mom worked hard and I had dance lessons twice a week, but I still found time for friends. June Riley and I ran around a lot together. We stayed in touch for a while after I left town but she moved from here when she got married three years ago and I didn't hear from her anymore."

"Denver Walton certainly looked like he wouldn't mind seeing you when I'm not around," he said as he tried to ignore a touch of jealousy.

She laughed. "You mean when Maddy isn't around.

She was giving me the evil eye, just like she used to do when we were in high school. Denver is a couple of years older than me but we went out on a couple of dates and Maddy and her friends treated me like I was a piece of dog poo stuck to her high heels. I guess they dated off and on through high school."

"They break up as often as a dog barks," Adam said with humor.

It was almost midnight when she held up her hand and pleaded sleepiness. He didn't offer to help her into the wheelchair, but rather watched with interest as she pulled it closer to where she sat, stood and balanced on her good foot, then pivoted into the chair.

"Thank you, Adam," she said once she was settled in the wheelchair.

"For what?" He also got up from the sofa.

"For bringing back my laughter, for giving me things to smile about. I had forgotten about happiness before you moved in here and you've brought some of that back to me."

"You're an amazing woman, Melanie. I know you'll figure out a way to do or be whoever you want."

She gazed at him ruefully. "I've already had seven months in this chair and I'm no closer to figuring that out than I was on my first day on wheels."

He smiled at her and pointed to the pictures on the wall. "Hopefully that was the last of your anger, or of you looking back and focusing on what you can't do. Now it's time to move forward and look at everything you can do."

She raised her chin and smiled, the gesture shooting

heat throughout his entire body. "You're right. It's time I really start thinking about all the things I'm capable of instead of dwelling on the one thing I can no longer do."

With her chin uplifted and a positive light spilling from her eyes, Adam wanted nothing more than to grab her up in his arms, carry her upstairs to his bed and make love to her.

But he hadn't forgotten how she'd stopped things from advancing on the night he stole a kiss from her. He remembered Nick's warning about breaking Melanie's heart, but he thought it far more likely that she was going to be his first real heartbreak.

Chapter 8

Was she insane? This was the thought that had raced through Melanie's head for the past couple of days. She hadn't been under the influence of her pills when the teakettle was misplaced, and her robe and nightgown hadn't been where they belonged. She hadn't taken any pain pills when she thought she'd received a strange phone call or on the night that she thought she'd seen somebody lurking in her front yard.

Had that simply been the work of her own madness? The desperate need of an invalid to create some sort of drama in her life?

Was it possible to have a mental snap from reality and not even know it? She stared down at the sketch pad on the kitchen table, but her thoughts were far away from anything she might have drawn.

Hadn't her mother mentioned at one time that she had a crazy aunt who wound up being institutionalized for hearing voices in her head? Was it possible that there was some mental illness gene inside her that had finally become active?

Was all of this just the beginnings of a total descent into madness? Maybe she should talk to a doctor…to a psychiatrist to see what was going on. Losing the use of her leg had been difficult, but believing she might possibly be losing her mind was horrible.

"You want me to make you something for dinner before I leave?" Tilly asked Melanie, who jumped at the sound of her voice.

"Gosh, Tilly, you scared me. I'd forgotten that you were in the house. And no, thanks. I'll just make myself a salad or something easy when I get hungry."

"Where's that man of yours today? He seems to be here underfoot most days."

"He's not my man and he drove into Evanston this afternoon to check out some things at the community college, and then I think he has one of his meetings tonight," Melanie replied.

Tilly leaned her skinny butt against the cabinets and gave Melanie a coy smile. "You know what the latest gossip is that's making the rounds?"

"I can't imagine," Melanie replied dryly.

"That you and Adam are lovers."

Despite her dark thoughts earlier about herself, a burst of laughter escaped Melanie. "Yeah, right, nothing like a one-legged woman to turn a man on."

"Half the men in this one-horse town would find

you sexy and beautiful one legged or two," Tilly replied fervently. "You just spend too much time holed up here all alone. You're beautiful from the inside out and the fact that you are in a wheelchair doesn't take any of that away from you. Besides, since Adam moved in here, you have a new sparkle in your eyes. Makes me wonder what's going on between the two of you when I'm not around."

Once again Melanie laughed. "Nothing. Absolutely nothing is going on," she replied. "We're enjoying a very nice friendship."

"Friends with benefits?" Tilly asked with another of her coy smiles.

"Tilly! Absolutely not." Melanie closed her sketchbook and smiled at Tilly.

Tilly grunted in dismay. "Too bad. I always did think that man was hot sin on two long legs."

"It wasn't that long ago you thought he was a serial killer chasing you down the stairs," Melanie reminded Tilly with a giggle.

Tilly's eyes widened. "Seriously, did you see how he looked with just that little towel wrapped around his waist? My goodness, if that wasn't a case of eye candy, I don't know what is."

For a moment Melanie's head filled with a vision of Adam hurrying down the stairs, the pale blue towel riding low on his slim hips. She sighed and turned the conversation toward the Halloween festivities the town had planned for the next week. She didn't want to talk about Adam Benson. She didn't even want to think about him.

"I heard that all the businesses along Main Street are going to stay open and give out candy in hopes of discouraging the children from going door to door anywhere else," Tilly informed her.

"That sounds like a good plan."

Tilly nodded. "It was Sheriff Evans's idea. That poor man has enough on his head with the two murders unsolved to have to worry about some kid going missing or getting lost going from farmhouse to farmhouse for treats."

"I'll need to get some candy. If all of Main Street is going to be open for business to ghosts and goblins, then I'll probably get some knocks on my door, as well."

"I'll pick up a big bag of candy and bring it with me the next time I stop by," Tilly said.

"No, that's not necessary. I'll get some from the store." Melanie thought about how easy it would be to take the ramp and wheel down the sidewalk to the grocery store a short block away.

The outing would do her good and she had a week to get up her nerve to actually accomplish it. Besides, it was time she got out more. Maybe that was her problem. She'd been cooped up for so long here, she was slowly going out of her mind, imagining bogeymen and phone calls and beating pictures on the wall to death.

The weather was supposed to go through a little warm-up in the next couple of days and she'd just plan a time to get out and buy the candy then.

"Are you sure?" Tilly asked. "I don't mind picking it up for you."

Melanie smiled. "I know, Tilly, but I need to start getting out and doing more things for myself."

Tilly nodded but tears suddenly appeared in her eyes. "I know. I want you to be independent but I just don't want you to stop needing me."

Melanie looked at her in surprise. "Tilly, you're like my second mother. I'll always need you in my life," she said softly. "I just don't need you to do so many things for me."

"You're changing," Tilly said, a hint of pride in her voice. "You're getting stronger and that's good. Your mother would be so proud of you, Melanie. I just want to make sure I'll always have a place in your life."

"That's a given," Melanie said gently.

Tilly nodded and straightened. "And now I'm going to finish the dusting upstairs so I can head out of here."

When she left the room, Melanie leaned back in her chair and thought about Tilly. Matilda Graves and Melanie's mother had been more like sisters than friends. Olive had never remarried after Melanie's father left and Tilly had never married at all.

Tilly had sat beside Melanie's mother at every dance recital Melanie had ever danced in, the two women had been together on the night of Melanie's prom and Tilly had grieved as deeply as Olive had when Melanie got on a plane to move to New York City to realize her dreams.

Within thirty minutes Tilly was gone and the evening stretched out before Melanie. She expected Adam to be gone until after she went to bed, and as she moved to the living room, she realized she'd come to look forward to his company whenever he was around.

He'd now officially been her tenant for two weeks, and with each day that passed, she found herself drawn to him more and more.

She didn't want to fall in love with him. She was even made uncomfortable by the fact that she liked him so much. Her cheeks warmed as she thought of the rumor that she and Adam were lovers.

The very idea was ridiculous. Or was it? There was no question that Adam felt a crazy desire for her, a desire born of close proximity, or of boredom or pity. It had to be one of those three.

She didn't believe his desire was anything real, but the desire she felt for him was very real. His kisses had stirred something in her that she'd never felt before.

But she also knew it was possible that her desire for him had been born from gratitude, and that if she followed through on it, he would eventually break her heart. Therefore she would deny him and herself any acting out on that passion. They shouldn't kiss again and she had to maintain some sort of emotional distance.

She was in a wheelchair and it was quite possible she was losing her mind. She would never be the kind of complete woman Adam would want or need in his life. No matter how self-sufficient she might eventually become, she would still always be a burden on any man.

Her mother had lived a full and happy life alone. Melanie would do the same. She'd rather be alone than allow somebody into her life who would eventually come to resent her for all her limitations.

Still, that didn't keep her from dreaming about

Adam, from occasionally falling into fantasies of what it would be like to make love with him.

In the living room she settled herself on the sofa and grabbed the remote to turn on the television. She tuned to a favorite crime drama show and for the next two hours lost herself in the world of actors and actresses in life-and-death situations.

By the time ten o'clock rolled around, her eyes were drifting closed with sleepiness and so she got back into her chair and went into her bedroom.

Her nightly routine of washing her face and changing into her nightclothes had become second nature to her and within minutes she was in bed, with the only light in the room the moonbeams drifting in through the window.

The light created dancing shadows on the ceiling and she watched them until she was half hypnotized and finally fell asleep.

Almost every night since the day she'd gone into the wheelchair, she'd dreamed of dancing, but on this night her dreams were filled with Adam.

She remembered how it had felt to be held in his arms as she cried, the warmth and strength of his embrace comforting and yet enticing and exciting.

The kisses they had shared had heated her body to the extent that she forgot all about the pain in her leg, the cold deadness in her foot. She'd felt completely alive and whole, and all she'd been able to think about was the fire of his kiss, which warmed her from head to toe and left her wanting more of him.

His hand as he stroked up and down the length of

her leg had pooled heat in her stomach, had warmed her blood, and she'd felt like an addict…wanting more… more.

Even in her dream she knew he was not hers to keep but was only borrowed for the time being, until he moved on. And he would move on.

If he decided to follow his dream and become a deputy, there was no work here in Grady Gulch. He'd have to leave town, start building a new life, and there was no way that life would include a nutty, crippled woman.

Still in her dreams he was in her bed, holding her, making love to her with blue fire in his eyes and hot passion on his lips.

She came awake suddenly and for a moment she thought it was an overwhelming sadness that had pulled her from her dreams. But it took her only an instant to realize it was something else.

A glance at the clock let her know she'd been sleeping for only an hour or so, but she had the strangest, craziest feeling that she was no longer alone in the room.

She told herself it was some sort of weird feeling left over from a half-remembered dream. Knowing that further sleep was unattainable, she sat up and leaned over to grab the arms of her wheelchair.

In stunned disbelief she realized her wheelchair wasn't there. But it should be there…where it always was when she got into bed.

Frantic, her state of half drowsiness jerking away, she shot her gaze around the room. She gasped as she saw the gleam of the metal chair in one corner of the room.

Dear God, had she gotten so crazy that she'd parked her wheelchair over there and somehow hobbled to her bed?

She clutched her hands on both sides of her head, wondering when this would all end…how this would all end for her. She was desperately afraid that not only would she never walk again, but she'd also wind up being locked up in some hospital for the insane.

Adam sat in the all-night café, nursing a cup of coffee and listening to some of his fellow AA members. He didn't always join them after the meeting for a cup of coffee or something to eat, but he'd decided to do so tonight.

He was still seeking a balance between wanting to be with Melanie and needing to get on with his own life. It was difficult, because he'd rather spend all of his time with her.

"Here we are," the waitress said as she placed a piece of warm apple pie in front of Adam and a slice of cherry in front of Jason Murray.

There were a total of four men who sat at the table. Jason Murray was a twenty-five-year-old who worked at a video store and had begun drinking when he was fifteen. Lawrence Connors was a fifty-year-old man who had finally realized he had a drinking problem after three failed marriages. Jack Rogers, the final member at the table, was about Adam's age and had also spent most of his time ranching. Too much isolation and too many lonely nights, Jack had confessed, were his reasons for drinking.

"I don't know why you keep coming to these meetings," Jason said to Adam as he cut into his pie. "We all know that you aren't like us, that alcohol isn't a driving demon in your head."

"Maybe I just come because I like the company," Adam countered.

Lawrence laughed. "Yeah, there's nothing that's as much fun as hanging out with a bunch of recovering alcoholics."

"Coming to the meetings is good for my soul," Adam replied easily. "It reminds me of how fragile all of us are and how we have to be accountable for what we do with our lives."

"I think if my old man had been around when I was growing up, I wouldn't have started drinking in the first place," Jason said.

"Accountability," Lawrence repeated firmly. "That's what we're talking about here. You're responsible for the choices you made, and whether your old man was in your life or not, you chose to raise a bottle to your mouth over and over again."

"You're right," Jason agreed and then smiled at the three older men. "But I'm also making the choice to get it right now."

"And we're all proud of you," Jack replied.

As they drank coffee and ate their pie, the conversation turned to normal man things…hunting, farming and sports. Adam always enjoyed these conversations, the subject matters ones he had often talked about with Sam and sometimes Nick.

Now Sam was incarcerated and Nick talked about

nothing but Garrett's funny antics and the charming little things that Courtney did. His life completely revolved around his family, as it should, but talking to Nick often made Adam feel very lonely.

He thought of the phone calls he'd resisted taking from Sam and the twelve steps of recovery. When he came to the step that called for each individual to take a personal inventory, he knew he fell short. He needed to let the judicial system take care of Sam, but more than that, Adam needed to forgive his brother.

As the others continued to talk, Adam found his thoughts drifting back to Melanie. He was worried about her. The thing with the pictures had unleashed a rivulet of both shock and sorrow through him.

Was she too damaged to move on and have a real life? Had the accident that had stolen her ability to dance taken out the very heart of her, leaving nothing left inside her?

He didn't want to believe that, but in the days since the picture incident she'd been almost impossible to read. She'd been so closed off, no hint of welcome in her eyes, whenever he was around.

In the time he was home, she either sat at the kitchen table, staring out the window, as if lost in thought, or was in her room alone.

Suddenly he was ready to head home…to her. She'd probably gone to bed long ago, but he would smell her scent when he walked through the front door, would feel her presence as he made his way up the stairs to go to sleep. Just knowing she was beneath the same roof as him somehow made him feel good.

"Gentlemen, it's been a pleasure as usual," Adam said as he stood. "But I've got a thirty-minute drive back home and it's way past my bedtime."

The others ribbed him good-naturedly and then Adam paid his tab and left the café. As he got into his truck for the drive back to Grady Gulch, his mind was filled with thoughts of both Sam and Melanie.

How could he make Melanie understand that she needed to somehow find a way to forgive the fates that had put her in a wheelchair when he couldn't even find forgiveness in his own heart for the brother he'd loved? For the man who, when their parents died, had stepped up and stepped in to make sure that all four siblings were able to remain together.

Sam had been barely an adult when he'd petitioned the court to gain custody of his three younger siblings. The idea of any of them going into foster care had been untenable to him.

He'd given up whatever hopes, whatever dreams he might have once entertained for himself to keep the ranch running and profitable, to manage his sister and brothers, who depended on him. He had sacrificed himself for them and finally had snapped.

A piece of brittle hardness against his brother cracked inside his chest and fell away. He would never condone what Sam had tried to do. He would never understand the rage and demons that had driven him to attempt to kill a woman, but he could forgive him for being sick.

Maybe it was time to let Sam know that Adam still

loved him. He vowed that the next time Sam tried to contact him, he'd take the call.

A lightness filled his heart with the decision, confirming that it was, indeed, the right decision, and as that particular subject left his mind, Melanie filled it once again.

He was getting in too deep with her, wanting her with a desire that had become a distraction each time they were together.

He knew he wasn't ready for a relationship, wasn't sure he'd ever be good husband material. But there was no question that Melanie made him think about such things. Something about her made him want to be a better man, to be good husband and father material.

Her laughter filled his heart with the music that was missing from her life. The strength and will she displayed in accomplishing all the things that other people took for granted awed him.

He'd never known anyone like her before, a woman who was both incredibly vulnerable and yet possessed a steely strength and a need for independence.

Yes, he was definitely getting too close to her. He awakened each morning with the firm commitment to gain some distance, but when they shared a breakfast or had a brief morning conversation, he found himself reluctant to leave.

He felt like a teenager enjoying his first real crush. He wanted to know what she was thinking, how she was feeling, at any given time of the day or night.

He was captivated by her sharp mind, entranced by

the sense of humor she'd only begun to display as they grew more comfortable together.

Even when she was sitting in her wheelchair, he found her incredibly sexy. Yeah, he was definitely developing a mad crush on his landlady. There was a part of him that wanted to follow through and see where things went between them and another part of him that believed doing so would be the biggest mistake of his life.

He clenched and then unclenched his hands around the steering wheel. Sometimes he thought his problem was that he ruminated on everything too much.

Sam had always made a decision and then stuck to it. Nick had led with his heart in every life choice he'd made, while Adam had always been the cautious one, carefully weighing the pros and cons until he felt frozen and too afraid to make any kind of meaningful decision.

He was finally beginning to trust his instincts, to go with his gut. Checking out the community college had felt right, and his desire to become a deputy felt just as right. He was finally on a course of action to become the man he wanted to be.

But, as much as he cared about Melanie, he was beginning to wonder if maybe she didn't need some sort of help that he couldn't give her. Maybe the illness that had made her leg useless had infected her soul to the point where nobody would ever be able to heal her.

Chapter 9

Melanie's brain worked to try to make sense of it, but there was no sense. Surely it was impossible that she'd left her chair by the window and then crawled into her bed. It simply wasn't physically possible, was it?

She didn't remember doing it, rather had the distinct memory of wheeling out of the bathroom and to the side of the bed. Was her memory faulty? Was she even crazier than she'd feared?

She was certain Adam hadn't sneaked in to do it. He would never play such a cruel trick on her. It simply wasn't in his character. So what was happening? What on earth was going on?

Terror tightened her throat as she heard a deep, heavy breathing that wasn't her own, felt an alien presence nearby. She wasn't alone. Somebody was definitely in the room with her.

"Adam?" she whispered softly, hopefully, as her heart banged painfully hard in her chest.

"Adam isn't home. Guess again." The deep, unfamiliar guttural voice came from the dark corner of the room opposite from where her wheelchair sat.

Alarm fired off in a dozen screams inside Melanie's head. "Who are you? What do you want?"

"It doesn't matter who I am. I'm here. You want your wheelchair? Crawl to it," he said and then laughed.

Sheer panic surged up inside her, choking her throat and for a long moment making her unable to draw a breath. Who was he? What was he doing here in her bedroom in the middle of the night? What did he want?

Was this the serial killer who had been stalking women in town? The man who had already murdered two women in their beds, slashing their throats while they slept? Was he here to make her his third victim?

A scream rose to her lips, but she knew she could scream her fool head off and it wouldn't do any good. Her house was sandwiched between businesses, businesses that had closed hours ago. She could scream, but there would be nobody close enough to hear her.

Still, she released a scream that pierced the night, that shrieked of the utter terror that possessed her as she realized the depth of danger around her.

Escape. The word thundered in her brain. She had to escape; she had to move. Somehow she had to get off the bed. She was a sitting duck here.

A sob escaped her lips. But how could she escape? She was crippled, unable to leap from the bed and run out of the room, unable to fight back when he decided to attack.

One thing was certain. She wasn't going to just sit around in the bed and wait for death to come to her. Drawing a deep breath, she rolled over and fell off the side of the bed and to the floor.

The man in the corner laughed again. "Like a fish out of water, flopping around on the floor."

She didn't recognize his voice, which he was obviously trying to disguise. She didn't even want to listen to him as he taunted her. Instead she focused on a plan formulating in her head.

The room was dark, and as long as he stood in the corner, teasing her, he couldn't see her as she used her arms and one good leg to move as silently as possible across the carpeted floor.

Ignoring rug burns and the ache of muscles scarcely used, she had only one goal in mind…to get into the closet. If she could just get inside the small enclosure, perhaps she could hold him off until Adam arrived back home.

The door to the closet was open slightly, just enough for her to grab it, slide in and pull it closed behind her. All she had to do was get there before he decided to stop talking and get serious.

"I can hear you slithering around on the floor like a snake," the voice said, this time sounding closer than it had seconds before.

With a new burst of terror, she increased her efforts, crawling backward like a crab as she dragged her bad leg across the floor. Three more feet. If she could just manage to go three more feet before he pounced, then she might be able to save herself.

All other thoughts left her head. She was aware of the man taunting her, getting closer and closer still, but her sole focus was on the closet.

Two more feet. Terror mingled with silent prayers as she pulled herself forward. *Help me! Somebody help me!* The words cried out inside her, but she knew nobody could help her but herself.

Another foot and her fingers touched the closet door. With Herculean effort she lurched backward and grabbed the door. With an outward gasp she pulled it open just enough for her to slink inside and then she closed the door and held the doorknob tight.

He laughed, and although there was something strangely familiar in the laughter, she couldn't identify it, couldn't identify him. "Looks like you've worked yourself into a dead end, Melanie."

She squeezed the doorknob tighter, her heart threatening to explode it was beating so fast. He knew her name. Who was it? This wasn't just a random stranger who had come into her house in the middle of the night, but rather somebody who knew her, knew her condition.

As she felt the knob attempt to turn beneath her grasp, she wondered where Adam was, if he would make it home in time to save her.

Somehow, someway, she realized, she had to save herself, but as the doorknob rattled again beneath her grip, she feared she wouldn't have the strength to keep the monster out of the closet.

* * *

By the time Adam reached Melanie's driveway, he was completely relaxed and ready for bed. He knew she'd already be asleep, for she rarely stayed up later than ten.

Time would tell what kind of help she needed, and if he might be the man to stand by her side when she got that help. He wasn't sure what was going on with her, but he knew with certainty that he wasn't ready to walk away from her yet. For the first time since he'd left his ranch, he felt needed. He just didn't know if she realized she needed, and wanted him yet.

He stepped outside of the truck and stretched with his arms overhead. The day had begun fairly mildly, but now a deep chill had taken over. Clouds chased across the front of the near full moon, half obscuring what should have been magnificent moonlight.

He shoved his hands in his pockets and jiggled the three chips inside. He'd received his third month of sobriety chip that night. He felt like a fraud when he was around the other men.

Since the day he'd stopped drinking, he'd never thought about it again, but he knew of the daily—sometimes minute-by-minute—struggles some of the others in the group suffered as they fought the battle of booze.

As he approached the front door, he heard the sound of muffled screams coming from someplace in the house. Panic jumped inside his veins and he fumbled with the key in an attempt to get the door unlocked as quickly as possible.

"Melanie?" he cried through the closed door, cursing his clumsiness as he tried to get the door open.

He finally opened it and stumbled into the dark interior, and as he took another step into the foyer, the screams became louder.

Melanie. His heart crashed against his ribs. "Melanie!" he shouted again. Had she fallen? Maybe taken a header in the shower? Was she seriously hurt?

He raced toward her bedroom and instantly flipped on the overhead light. In the blink of an eye he took in the scene before him, trying to make sense of it all.

The street-level window was open, the screen missing, and her wheelchair had been pushed into one corner of the room. Melanie wasn't in it or in the bed.

The screams had stopped and in the silence Adam could hear the banging of his own heartbeat as a panic like he'd never known before roared through him. Where was she? What had happened while he'd been gone?

The screams began again, sobbing, terror-filled screams, and he realized they were coming from the closet. He raced to the door and attempted to turn the knob, but it refused to turn in his hand.

"Go away! Leave me alone!" Melanie's voice sounded hoarse and yet was filled with such fear, it ripped through his heart. She screamed again.

"Melanie, it's me," he said. "It's Adam. Let me open the door. It's okay. You're safe. I'm here."

A deep, wrenching sob sounded, and when he tried to turn the doorknob again, it turned easily in his hand.

He pulled the door open to find her crumpled on the floor like a broken doll.

"I woke up and he was in my room." The words came haltingly out of her, punctuated by hiccuping sobs. "He moved my wheelchair. I slid off the bed and crawled in here. I held the doorknob tight so he couldn't open it. He was going to kill me. I know that's what was going to happen." Her sobs made the words half gibberish, but Adam definitely got enough information to realize what had apparently happened.

She burst into a new fit of tears as Adam bent down and picked her up. She slung her arms around his neck and buried her face in the crook of his neck, her entire body trembling uncontrollably.

She was nearly weightless in his arms and so achingly fragile, Adam's blood ran cold as he gently laid her on her bed. It was now obvious what had happened. Somebody had come through the window while she slept, somebody who could only have had evil intent.

He chilled as he thought of what might have happened to her if he'd lingered another minute over his piece of pie, if he hadn't driven a little over the speed limit coming home. How much longer could she have held on to the closet doorknob? And what would have happened if the intruder had managed to open that door? His heart iced at the very possibilities.

He sank next to her on the bed and stroked her hair as her tears began to ebb. "I was so afraid," she said with a final gasping sob. "I thought I was going to be just like those other women, like the waitresses. I thought he was going to kill me in my bed." Her body trembled with such a force he held tight, as if in doing so, he was holding her together.

"We need to call Cameron," he finally said as her trembling began to subside. "We need to report this."

Her eyes were huge as she slowly nodded her head. "Do you think it was the serial killer? Was I supposed to be his next victim?" Her voice was unusually deep and raspy, both from screaming and from the intense emotion that still coursed through her body.

"Anything is possible," Adam said tersely as he pulled his cell phone from his pocket and punched in the number for the sheriff.

Melanie wrapped her arms around her shoulders as if in an attempt to fight off a shiver that began in her very soul.

As Adam waited for Cameron to answer the call, he felt the same kind of shiver attempt to take hold of him as he realized that danger had crept not only into the house but into Melanie's bedroom while she slept.

It took him only minutes to reach the sheriff and give a quick assessment of the situation and request assistance. When he hung up the phone, he tucked it back into his pocket and moved away from Melanie.

"Sit tight," he said to her. "I'm just going to get your robe." There was no way in hell he wanted the sheriff or any of the deputies to see Melanie in her sexy blue nightgown.

"It's hanging on the back on my bathroom door," she said. Her voice sounded a little bit stronger, as if some of the shock was slowly wearing off.

He found the white terry-cloth robe just where

she'd told him it would be, and carried it back into her bedroom. He helped her into it and then once again wrapped his arms around her.

He didn't ask her any questions and she didn't offer any more information. She simply clung to him as if he were a lifeline.

The idea that anyone would try to put their hands on her in an effort to harm her shot rage through him.

"I didn't do this to myself," she whispered.

He leaned back and looked at her in surprise. "It never crossed my mind that you did."

"Maybe somebody will think I'm just some poor crippled woman looking for attention, that I tore the screen off the window, left my wheelchair in the corner and then crawled into the closet and waited for you to come home." A new sob welled up and spilled from her lips.

"Melanie, stop," he protested.

She looked up at him with eyes that simmered with emotion. "Isn't that what you think? That I'm just a poor little cripple?"

"Never," he replied truthfully. "And you need to get that thought out of your head. We need to get you into the living room. The sheriff should be here anytime."

She swiped at the tears that had begun to fill her eyes once again. "Can you bring me my chair?"

He started for it and then halted in his tracks. "We need to leave it where it is. Maybe there are fingerprints on it that will let us know who was in here."

He walked back to where she sat on the bed and scooped her up in his arms. Once again she wrapped her arms around his neck and leaned into him. For a moment he imagined that he could feel her heartbeat matching the rhythm of his own.

"It's going to be all right, Melanie," he promised. "I'm here and I'm going to make sure everything is all right." He just hoped it was a promise he could keep.

By the time Sheriff Cameron Evans arrived on scene with two of his deputies, Melanie was tightly wrapped in her fuzzy winter robe and seated on the sofa. The chill that she'd felt since the moment she realized somebody was in her bedroom with her had ebbed somewhat, replaced by a half-numb feeling.

Somebody had intended to kill her. Why? Was it the serial killer who had been in the bedroom with her? Everything now had a surreal feel to it.

Adam paced the floor in front of her, sighing in relief as the lawmen finally arrived.

"What's going on?" Cameron asked as he stepped into the living room, followed closely behind by Deputies Jim Collins and Ben Temple. "Your call was too frantic for me to know for sure what had happened."

"Somebody tried to kill me." The words fell from Melanie's mouth and sent a new wave of icy chills up and down her back.

"Where?" Cameron stood at attention, his eyes narrowed in fierce concentration, as Adam sat down next to Melanie and took one of her cold hands in his.

"I was asleep and something woke me up." She squeezed Adam's hand as the horror of the events she'd experienced replayed in her mind. "At first I thought it was just a dream that had awakened me, but when I went to reach for my wheelchair, it wasn't there, and then I saw it across the room, in the corner."

She shuddered, remembering that moment of utter helplessness. "And then I knew somebody was in the room with me. It was a man, and he told me if I wanted the wheelchair I had to crawl to it."

"Did you recognize the voice?" Adam asked.

She hadn't told him about the man speaking to her before Cameron had arrived. She shook her head. "It was like he was trying to disguise it, but when he laughed, I thought something about it was vaguely familiar."

"So you think it was somebody you know?" Cameron said.

She hesitated a moment and then shrugged her shoulders. "I can't be one hundred percent sure, but he knew me. He called me by name."

For the next few minutes she told Cameron exactly what had happened, everything the man had said to her and how she'd managed to get off the bed and get into the closet, where she'd held on tight to the knob as he'd tried to open the door.

By the time she finished, Adam's grip on her hand was almost painfully tight and yet she welcomed the ache, a confirmation that she'd survived the night, the terror.

"You two sit tight. We're going to check out the bedroom," Cameron said. He and the two men disappeared into the bedroom and Adam released her hand and then wrapped his arm around her shoulder and pulled her more tightly against his side.

"You could have been killed," he said, his voice deep and filled with a wealth of emotion. "If you hadn't been smart enough to get off the bed and into the closet, he would have attacked you."

"I didn't know what else to do," she replied. "I knew if I remained on the bed, I didn't have a chance." She frowned and smacked her right thigh, as if to punish it. "I couldn't exactly get up and run away." An old bitterness crept into her tone. "He probably broke into my room because he knew that I was nothing more than a helpless cripple."

Adam placed his hand beneath her chin and forced her to meet his gaze. "Melanie, you're so much more than that and you proved it tonight. You outwitted a man. You saved yourself from danger."

She looked at him doubtfully. "I don't know how much longer I could have held on to that doorknob. If you hadn't come home when you did, I think he would have managed to get the closet door open. He would have managed to get to me."

"But the important point is that you hung on as long as you had to."

She leaned back against him, finding strength in the warmth of his arm around her, in the admiration that shone from his eyes.

He shouldn't admire her. She'd managed only to keep herself safe until he rode to her rescue. If he'd arrived five minutes later, she probably would have been stretched out on her bed with her throat slashed.

"I think Cameron had hoped that whoever killed the other two women was a drifter who moved out of town, since nothing else has happened in this last three months," Adam said.

"I guess this throws that theory out the window," she replied.

She had felt like she was making progress, finally seeking some sort of acceptance concerning her medical condition. But being helpless for those tense seconds on the bed had slammed her handicap home to her once again.

She'd probably been chosen as a victim because she was weak and useless. Would he have broken into her bedroom if she were a healthy, active twenty-eight-year-old instead of a pathetic cripple? She didn't think so.

She'd never been so scared and she'd never felt so low, and she knew the only reason why Adam was beside her now was that he'd been pulled into her drama by being her tenant.

"You know, if you want to move to a place with a little less stress and drama, I'd understand," she said softly.

"I'm not going anywhere, Melanie," he said firmly. "I haven't done anything to void our lease and you haven't done anything to give me reason to want to move out. I'm happy just where I am." He offered her a small smile. "Besides, I forgot to mention to you that I thrive on stress and drama."

She sighed in relief. At least for now he was here with her, beside her, lending her his strength and support. She had no idea what tomorrow might bring but at this moment in time what he had to give her was exactly what she needed.

She straightened and Adam stood as Cameron came back into the living room. "Ben and Jim are processing things, looking for fibers or fingerprints, and I've called in a couple of other men to canvass the neighborhood to see if anyone saw anything. In the meantime I'd like to ask you some more questions."

"Okay," she agreed. She laced her fingers in her lap, aware that the cold that encased her heart radiated down to her fingertips.

"Is there anyone in town you've had a beef with? Somebody you know who doesn't like you?" Cameron asked as he eased down in the chair opposite the sofa, a pad and pen in his hand. Adam remained standing next to the sofa, as if ready to leap to Melanie's defense if it should become necessary.

"The first few months I was here and in the wheelchair, I wasn't the most pleasant person in the world," she admitted. "But my interaction with anyone was very limited."

"Until the other night, when we went to the Cowboy Café," Adam said.

Cameron's eyes darkened. "The Cowboy Café. Did you see anyone there in particular? Anyone pay extra attention to you?"

"Not really. There were some people who came up to me to say hello, people who didn't realize I was here in town." She frowned thoughtfully, trying to imagine anyone who might want to hurt her.

"Craig Jenkins has been giving her a hard time," Adam said.

"The real estate guy from Evanston?"

"Initially when I came back here to spend my mother's last days with her, I contacted him to make arrangements to sell the house. I just assumed I'd be returning to New York City, but then I went into the wheelchair and knew I wouldn't be returning to my previous life, so I told him I was no longer interested." Melanie grimaced with displeasure. "He didn't want to take no for an answer and became a real pest."

"I had a stern little talk with him last week and told him to leave her alone, that they had no business to conduct," Adam admitted. The sound of a small vacuum sweeper whirled from in the bedroom.

Cameron bent his head and wrote for a moment on his pad and then looked from Adam to Melanie. "Anyone else?"

"Denver Walton seemed unusually happy to see her," Adam added.

Melanie laughed, surprised that she still could under the circumstances. "Maddy Billings would be more apt to murder me in my bed than Denver, and the person in my room was definitely a man."

"I don't know if this means anything or not but you might want to check out Kevin Naperson's alibi. He helped me put up some railings on the ramp, and he probably knows by now about Melanie being handicapped."

Cameron frowned. "That kid seems to wind up someplace in every investigation." Once again he scribbled on his pad and then looked up again at Melanie. "Did you leave any broken hearts behind when you left New York City?"

An unexpected burst of laughter escaped her once again. "Not that I'm aware of. It was well over a year since I'd dated anyone before I came back here."

"What about when you left here years ago?" It was obvious by the question that Adam was desperate to make sense of what had happened.

"What about that?" Cameron asked.

She shrugged. "I didn't date anyone really seriously before I left for New York. Denver and I went out a couple of times in high school. I dated Billy Vickers for about a month. Even Jim and I went out a few times."

"Jim Collins?" Cameron asked in surprise.

She nodded. "But that was a long time ago and none of those relationships were serious ones. Everyone knew that as soon as I graduated from high school, I was heading out of town. It wasn't a big secret that I had the stars of Broadway in my eyes."

She glanced down at her leg, a new sense of betrayal slicing through her. She drew a deep sigh and stared at Cameron.

"Has there been anything else strange happening in your life?" he asked.

Adam looked at the pictures on the wall, all of them void of glass. "The photo glass was broken on all the pictures."

Cameron raised a sandy eyebrow as Adam explained about the peculiar event.

"I thought I had done it in my sleep," she admitted.

"Nothing was stolen? No sign of forced entry anywhere in the house?" Cameron asked.

"We didn't really look around. I think I convinced Adam that I was responsible for it, but now I'm not so sure. I certainly don't remember doing it, but it was apparently done in the middle of the night."

A combination of relief and new fear shot through her. If she hadn't broken the pictures, then that meant somebody else had been in her house that night and that also meant she wasn't losing her mind. What was frightening was the idea that somebody had come and gone from her house, moving things, touching things, somebody who didn't belong and had no reason to be there.

Cameron leaned back in the chair, looking as weary as a man could look and still be alive. At that time Ben and Jim entered the living room.

"The screen was removed from the outside and the window was opened, but whoever did it left no fingerprints behind," Jim said. "Must have worn gloves."

"I vacuumed around the window, in the corners and around the bed and the outside of the closet, but I didn't see anything substantial," Ben said as he hefted the small vacuum he'd carried in with him. "I'll get the contents checked at the lab and see if we can come up with anything."

Melanie looked at all the men and she knew what they were all thinking but not saying. "The man who sneaked into my bedroom while I slept, he was probably the same person who killed Candy Bailey and Shirley Cook, wasn't he?"

Cameron's frown deepened and he gave a curt nod

of his head, a nod that once again caused fear to shudder through Melanie. "Yeah, I think it's possible it's the same perp. Did you know Candy or Shirley? Have any kind of interaction with either of them?"

"No to both questions. So what happens now?" she asked, aware her voice sounded tiny and afraid, just like she felt at the moment.

Cameron stood from the chair. "To be honest, I don't know. We'll investigate to the best of our ability, but as far as I know, you're the first woman who has survived an attack by this guy. I don't know if that means he'll go for another target or he'll stay focused on you in an attempt to finish what he started."

If Melanie was seeking some sort of reassurance from the sheriff, it was definitely not going to happen. As she caught and captured Adam's gaze, she saw the fear that lit his eyes and knew that fear was for her.

Chapter 10

It was two o'clock in the morning and Adam and Melanie sat at the kitchen table, drinking coffee and waiting for the residual adrenaline of the night to finally pass.

The officers had left, any evidence that might have been collected had been carried away and Adam had double-checked every window and door in the house to make sure they were all locked up tight.

"I can't believe I didn't hear the window open," she said as she cupped her fingers around her mug. "I'm not even sure what woke me up."

"I can't believe you didn't have the window locked," Adam chided.

"I guess I got lazy," she admitted. "But, trust me, I won't be lazy again. When I think of what might have happened if I hadn't awakened…" She shook her head and frowned. "This whole place is going to stay locked up like Fort Knox from now on." Her eyes held a haunting darkness that he knew only time would take away.

She took a sip of her coffee and then set the mug back on the table. "I guess I thought I was safe because I wasn't a waitress at the Cowboy Café, because I had no ties to the place."

"Despite the fact that the first two murder victims worked at the café, I don't think Cameron was ever tied completely to the theory that the deaths were specifically about the people at the café. The evidence shows that Candy Bailey might have invited her killer into the cabin where she was staying, and Shirley Cook's killer came in through an open window in her living room. Cameron believes the killings were ones of convenience, of victim availability, rather than specifically tied to the café."

"So I played right into his hands by having my bedroom window unlocked."

"That's what I would guess," he replied.

She frowned and looked out the kitchen window, where the darkness of night was complete. "It's hard to believe that somewhere out there a man is wandering the streets, checking out homes to find an easy access to a woman he can kill."

"I think the most difficult thing to fathom is that this man is one of us, somebody we might stand next to in line at the grocery store or someone who might sit at the booth next to us at the café. This isn't just some crazed stranger who has drifted into town, but rather this man is one of us."

"Know any crazies in town?" she asked with a forced lightness.

He leaned back in his chair, taking her question seriously. "I know a lot of people I consider slightly odd. I find it odd that old man George Wilton eats at the café every day and yet complains about how bad the food is there. I find it odd that Thomas Manning arrived in town a year ago and the only time he's seen is when he goes to the café for a meal and reads while he eats."

Adam frowned, wondering if Cameron had ever looked closely at Thomas, who was a relative newcomer to the area. Nobody had been murdered before his arrival. "But odd doesn't a murderer make."

"I think it's safe to assume that he's the one who broke the pictures and moved my things around. That means he was in the house before tonight. Do you think he'll come back here again?" Her voice was small and trembled slightly as she once again picked up her mug and held it between her hands.

"I'd love to be able to tell you no with real certainty, but I can't. I can't begin to imagine what he'll do next. I don't know if he'll seek out a new victim or come back here for you." He leaned forward. "But one thing is clear. I'm going to make sure you stay safe. I'll bunk down here on the sofa so that I can hear if anyone tries to enter the house from the lower level."

"I'm just surprised he decided to choose me since you live here with me." She took another sip of her coffee but kept the mug between her hands. "I mean, from what I understand, both Candy Bailey and Shirley Cook lived alone."

"Tonight my truck wasn't out front, where it normally is parked. He knew you were in here all alone." A surge of anger welled up in Adam. "He must have been watching...waiting for the opportunity when I'd be gone."

Her eyes were almost black as she held his gaze. "I truly thought I was losing my mind, that somehow I was going insane. I don't know what's worse, going crazy or knowing that some killer has come and gone through my bedroom window as if he was an invited guest. I guess I sleep more soundly than I thought I did."

Adam sat up straighter in his chair. "There won't be anyone coming in through that window again. If it makes you feel better, I'll completely board up that window to make sure not even a teensy fly can make its way inside."

Adam's blood ran a little bit colder as he pictured the intruder entering the house to break the photos and erase a caller ID number from her phone. He'd obviously come in while Melanie slept on a number of occasions. Why hadn't he killed her then? It made no sense.

"Who would want to make you believe you're going crazy?" he asked.

She laughed, the sound holding no real merriment. "I can't imagine." The smile fell from her lips. "Why would somebody make me want to think I'm insane?"

"I don't know." He gazed at her speculatively. "If you die, what happens to this house?"

She looked at him in surprise. "I'm not sure. I have no heirs and I'm paying off some back taxes my mother owed, so I guess it would just go up for auction." Her eyes narrowed as she obviously followed his trail of thought. "Which would make it very easy for Craig to get it for next to nothing."

"Maybe this really wasn't the serial killer. Maybe it was Craig trying to hurry things along," Adam speculated. "There's no question that this house could be prime commercial property after simple rezoning."

Melanie shrugged. "I don't think it makes much of a difference who kills me. Dead is dead."

"For sure," he agreed. "But we aren't going to let that happen. I'm going to mention all of this to Cameron and make sure he checks out Craig's alibi for tonight."

He could tell she was getting tired. Her shoulders had begun to slump and the tension that had wafted off her all night was slowly dissipating.

"Maybe we should call it a night." He got up and carried his mug to the sink. "I'm just going to go upstairs and get a pillow and a blanket and I'll be right back down."

She nodded absently as her gaze once again went to the darkness outside the window.

He took the stairs two at a time, wondering if he'd ever be able to forget the sound of her screams, the terror that had lit her eyes as he'd finally managed to pull her out of the closet.

He didn't want to think about how close tragedy had come. There had already been too much tragedy in his life. He'd lost his parents and his sister and Sam. He didn't want to lose her, too.

It took him only moments to grab a pillow from his bed and find an oversize fleece blanket in the hall closet. He grabbed the handgun from the top shelf of the closet, where he'd placed it when he'd moved in, and carried them all downstairs. He threw the pillow and blanket on the sofa, placed his gun on the coffee table and then went back into the kitchen to find her still seated at the kitchen table.

"Are you going to be all right?" he asked softly.

She jerked, as if his voice had startled her, and then offered him a hesitant smile. "I'll just be glad when this night passes and the sun shines again."

He watched as she moved away from the table and carried her mug to the dishwasher. Once she'd loaded it, she followed Adam into the living room but halted just outside her bedroom door, her eyes once again dark and filled with a hint of fear.

"You have a gun?" Her gaze was locked on the weapon on the coffee table.

"I do. Does it bother you?"

She nibbled on her lower lip, her gaze remaining on the gun. When she finally looked back at him, there was a hint of a cold resolve in her eyes. "No, it doesn't bother me at all."

"I'll be right here with the gun," he said and sat on the sofa to prove his point. "Somebody would have to get through me to get to you."

She nodded and then wheeled herself into the bedroom. Adam waited until he saw the illumination from the lamp next to her bed and then he unfolded the blanket and prepared to lie down, even though he knew sleep would be a long time coming, if at all.

He took off his shirt and then shucked his jeans, deciding his boxers and his gun could handle anything that might go awry for the rest of the night.

The light in her room was turned off as he placed his head on the pillow and pulled the fleece blanket on top of him. All the what-ifs in the world took possession of his thoughts.

If he hadn't stopped to have that pie and visit with the men, would he have managed to get here in time to catch the perpetrator? God, he would have loved to have that man close enough to wrap his hands around his throat, to squeeze until his eyes bulged with the same kind of fear he'd instilled in Melanie.

If he'd lingered over another cup of coffee, if he'd driven slower than he had, would the perp have managed to drag Melanie from the closet? Would Adam have come home to find Melanie dead in her bed?

A surge of protectiveness he'd never before experienced in his life swelled in his chest. He wanted to keep her safe, not just for her sake, but also for his own.

He couldn't imagine not seeing her smile the first thing every morning. In the short time he'd been living here, he'd become accustomed to her face, her laughter and her beauty, both inside and out.

He released a sigh, recognizing that the adrenaline that had driven him since he'd arrived home earlier was finally beginning to ebb.

He'd just started to nod off when he heard Melanie call his name. Instantly tension coursed through him. He grabbed his gun and hit the light switch as he stumbled into her room.

Danger! His brain registered it, but it was not the

kind of danger he'd anticipated. There was no stranger in the room, no sign of any trouble—except the trouble that might come from an instantaneous burst of desire.

Danger sat in the center of the king-size bed, her shiny blond hair slightly tousled and her midnight-blue nightgown with spaghetti straps exposing far too much of her creamy skin. Danger came in the darkness of her blue eyes and the whisper of a tentative smile that curved her lips.

He lowered his gun to his side. "You called me?"

She averted her gaze from him as a faint pink stained her cheeks. "I'm embarrassed to admit it, but I'm still afraid. I was wondering if maybe you wouldn't mind bunking in here with me just for tonight." She scooted over to the edge of the bed and gestured to the empty space beside her.

She was going to kill him, he thought. It was going to kill him to sleep next to her on that bed, with her scent dizzying his head and his desire thrumming through his veins. Still, there was no question that he was going to do what she needed, even if it did kill him.

There was no question that the moment Melanie had gotten into bed, the fear of that moment when she had awakened and knew she wasn't alone in the room returned full force.

She tried to shove it back, telling herself she was safe, that there was nothing to worry about. Adam was in the next room, on the sofa, and he'd said he would hear anything that might portend trouble.

Still, it wasn't enough. Her breathing became painful

and her heart banged with a flashback of those moments of utter terror. She wanted to be strong. She wanted to be okay alone, but she wasn't.

When she called his name and he appeared in her room, clad in a pair of dark blue boxers and clutching a gun, she recognized she didn't want him in her bed just to make her feel secure. She wanted him in her bed with his arms wrapped around her, with his lips pressed to hers. She wanted him to make her feel alive and vital and whole by stroking her naked body.

"Whatever you need from me, Melanie," he finally said.

She reached out and turned on the bedside lamp despite the fact that the overhead light illuminated the room. He flipped the switch that turned off that light and in the glow of the lamp walked around to the opposite side of the bed.

He placed his gun on the nightstand and then got into the bed and under the sheet, keeping his body so close to the edge that she knew if she breathed hard, he'd fall off the bed and hit the floor.

For several long minutes they remained that way, tension a third occupant between them in the bed. "Are you comfortable?" she asked, finally breaking the silence.

"Sure. I'm fine." He was obviously lying through his teeth. "What about you? Feel better with me in here?"

She hesitated before replying, weighing the pros and cons of what she wanted and what would be best for both of them. She had no illusions of any happily ever after with Adam or with any other man. If she encouraged him tonight to make love to her, it changed nothing.

Except she would have a single sweet, hot memory to carry her through the years. Could she live with that? Would a memory be enough? Probably not, but it would be better than no memory at all.

She turned to face him, his features barely discernible in the moonlight that filtered in through the window. "Actually, I don't feel much better. I think it would help if you moved a little closer to me."

She didn't want to actually come out and ask him for what she wanted. She wanted him to need her as much as she did him. She wanted to let him know that she was extending an invitation, but she didn't want to be the one to answer it for him. She wanted him to make a move on her because he couldn't stand not to, because his desire for her overwhelmed his common sense.

He moved an inch closer, still too far away for them to even accidentally bump into one another. "Is that better?" he asked.

"Maybe it would ease my mind if you could move close enough to put your arm around me." She held her breath as she waited for his reply.

A small deep moan escaped him. "I have to tell you, I want to do what you need, Melanie, but you're playing with fire here."

As he moved closer, close enough that his body warmed her side and he gathered her into his arms, she closed her eyes and relaxed against him. "Playing with fire?" she said softly.

"A roaring inferno," he replied gruffly. He'd whispered the words against the back of her ear and she fought against a shiver of excitement. "Melanie, I haven't been able to stop thinking about kissing you. I haven't been able to stop thinking about the softness of your skin beneath my hands. I'm not going to lie. I want you. I want you in a way that's slowly killing me inside."

They were the words she'd longed to hear, words that chased away the fear that the night had held, promising to replace it with something wonderful, something beautiful.

"I want you, too." She turned over in his arms and faced him.

"I don't want to hurt you."

"Unless you intend to eat my foot, there's no way you're going to hurt me," she replied with a touch of humor. "Adam, don't treat me like an invalid. Treat me like the fully functioning woman that I am."

She barely got the words out of her mouth before his lips touched hers. Gently at first, his lips teased and tormented, until finally she opened her mouth to encourage him to deepen the kiss.

And he did, his tongue delving inside to battle with hers as a roar of excitement resounded in her head. His arms tightened around her as the fire in his kiss half stole her breath away.

It had been so long, so achingly long since she'd felt wanted and the passion in his kiss soothed some of the jagged edges that had been inside her since the day she lost her ability to walk.

In bed with him it didn't matter that she couldn't

walk. They were equals as they lay prone in each other's arms, drinking their fill of each other with their mouths.

He kissed with a natural mastery that thrilled her, and when his hand stroked down her back along the slick material of her nightgown, it warmed each place it lingered. She arched against his palm, like a cat needing to be scratched.

And she needed to be scratched. She needed to be scratched and stroked and loved until she forgot that she was damaged goods, until she forgot that there would never be a man permanently in her life. She needed this night with Adam. Just this single night was all she asked for.

As he finally pulled his mouth from hers, she stroked down his strong chest, loving the feel of his hot skin and beating heart.

He moved his mouth down the column of her neck, nipping and teasing with his lips against her sensitive skin. She fought a shiver as his mouth found her collarbones and skimmed across them to slide lower…lower until his mouth captured the tip of her breast over the silk nightgown.

She hissed at the erotic feel of the material heating beneath his mouth. Her nipples grew taut as he moaned deep in the back of his throat.

His hands covered her breasts as his mouth found hers again, this time in a kiss that screamed of passion unleashed. He was close enough to her that she could feel his erection pressing against her hip.

Her. He wanted her. If there had been any doubt in her mind, it was banished by the physical evidence of his desire. Suddenly she wanted the few clothes that remained a barrier between them gone.

She sat up and he did, as well, and she knew he had no idea why she'd halted what was happening. She reached down to the bottom of her gown and worked it up her body, exposing the pale pink bikini panties she wore before she finally pulled the gown over her head and tossed it to the floor.

He remained sitting up next to her, his eyes glittering like a wild animal's in the spill of moonlight. "You are so beautiful," he said, his voice filled with a reverent awe. "You take my breath away like nobody has ever done before."

She smiled as wave after wave of pleasure stole through her. "I hope you have enough breath to take off those boxers, because I want to feel you naked against me."

These words spurred him into action. He ripped off his boxers as if they were filled with fire ants and she pulled off her bikini panties. He rolled over to once again take her in his arms.

She reveled in their skin-to-skin contact. As they began to explore each other's bodies, she quickly learned that if she touched his inner thigh, he groaned, and if she gently raked her fingernails across his back, he moaned.

And it didn't take him long to discover that a stroke up her inner thigh made her tremble with anticipation, that his mouth latched on to one of her nipples caused her to tangle her hands in his hair and emit sweet sounds of pleasure.

Hesitant touches became more sure, and their passion grew in intensity, making them both breathless and frantic with need. He moved to the side of her and with a hand caressed her stomach, down to the place where she needed him, wanted him most.

As he found her sweet spot and began to move his fingers lightly against her flesh, a rising tide of intense pleasure drove everything out of her head except the need to ride the wave. Her hands clenched the bedsheets on either side of her as his mouth covered hers, breathing in her gasps and moans of mindless need.

And then she was there, on top of the wave, riding it out until her body shattered apart and she was boneless and mindless.

As her senses began to return, she reached down and circled his engorged hardness with her hand. A swift intake of breath was her response.

"Don't," he said urgently. "If you touch me anymore, I'll explode, and I suddenly realized I don't have any protection with me." Frustration rang in his voice.

"I'm on the pill," she said, "and I don't sleep around. It's okay, Adam. Please, just make love to me."

Her words obviously satisfied him, for he moved on top of her and positioned himself between her thighs. He hesitated only a moment. As she grabbed his buttocks in her hands and arched beneath him, he moved forward, plunging himself into her.

She cried out with the sheer wonder of their connection and for a long moment neither of them moved. He hovered above her, his neck muscles taut and his eyes closed. He looked beautiful, and her heart swelled so big, it made it difficult for her to breathe.

As he began to move against her, into her, she found her air, and she gasped again and again as he slid deeper and deeper with each thrust.

She wanted him deep, deeper still, and she raised her legs upward. Her action stopped him and he stared down at her, as if amazed that she could move her legs at all.

His stunned surprise lasted only a second and then he moved his hips once again. The friction of their bodies thrusting together created a new wave inside her, a wave greater than the one before.

She cried out as she felt the wave coming closer… closer still and he cried her name in response. She was drowning in pleasure as the force of her climax washed over her and she was vaguely aware of him stiffening against her with his own release.

He collapsed to the side of her, his breathing still rapid but beginning to slow. She matched her breaths to his until they both were breathing in a normal rhythm.

He rolled over on his side to look at her. "That was beyond amazing."

"I was thinking along the lines of earth-shattering," she replied.

His laugh was a low rumble, which she felt in the pit of her stomach. "I like that." He paused and then continued, "I didn't know you could move your leg."

"Most of the damage is from the thigh down. I have little mobility of the leg. I just can't stand and I can't feel my foot. That makes crutches pretty much out of the question."

The subject of her foot stanched some of the happiness she'd momentarily felt. "I'll be right back," she said as she pulled herself out of the bed and into the wheelchair.

The seat of the chair felt particularly cold against her bare butt as she reached down and grabbed her nightgown from the floor and then wheeled herself into the bathroom. Once there she freshened up, avoiding her reflection in the mirror that hung on the back of the door.

She knew it was ridiculous, but the question about her foot had been a slam back into reality. She was a cripple, and while she could make love with abandon, she would never, ever be the woman that Adam Benson needed in his life.

Chapter 11

It was just after five the next morning when Adam got out of bed and left her bedroom. Although he hated to wash off the scent of her that lingered on his skin, he went upstairs and quickly showered and dressed for the day.

Back in the kitchen he made coffee, and then, with a cup in hand, he went to stand at the window that looked out on the backyard. The sun was just beginning to peek over the horizon, shooting out a pink glow that promised a clear, beautiful autumn day.

As he sipped his coffee, his thoughts were filled with the woman who still slept in the bed nearby. He'd done something wrong. He'd completely ruined the moment. After they'd made love, he shouldn't have asked her about her foot. Somehow he'd broken the mood, chased away any further intimacy that might have occurred when she returned to the bed, clad in her nightgown, and told him she was tired.

She'd curled up on her side away from him and after a few minutes of silence he'd grabbed his boxers and gone into the bathroom.

When he'd returned to the bed, she'd pretended to be asleep, and that had been the end of things. It had taken him forever to finally fall asleep, as the events of the night played and replayed through his mind.

It had been a roller coaster of a night, first the horror of the attack on Melanie and then the joy of making love to her and finally the disconnect he'd felt when she returned to the bed. He'd definitely screwed up after they made love.

He'd gotten only a couple of hours of sleep, but he felt refreshed, invigorated and eager to touch base with Cameron to see what he'd found out during the night.

Adam wasn't sure what to believe about the attack. It was possible she'd been targeted by the serial killer, but it was equally possible Craig Jenkins had tried to scare her badly enough that she'd want to sell this place and leave Grady Gulch forever.

His hand tightened around his coffee cup as he thought of the squirrelly little real estate man. How far would he go to achieve his goal of buying what could be considered prime real estate?

Why would anyone want to make Melanie believe she was losing her mind? Was it possible Craig had been playing mind games with her to have her institutionalized and then he could move in and somehow take possession of the house? Would he actually kill her to achieve his goal?

Certainly money was a universal motive for murder, but so were passion and jealousy and revenge. Was it Craig? Or was Adam missing something?

His phone rang and he quickly fumbled it from his pocket, not wanting it to awaken Melanie. When he saw the caller ID, he paused. The call was from the Oklahoma City jail.

It was Sam.

He hesitated a moment and then took the call. It was relatively brief and painful, but when it was finished, Adam was grateful that the ice that had encased his heart where Sam was concerned had melted a bit.

It was almost eight when Melanie made an appearance in the kitchen. She smelled like minty soap and a touch of floral perfume and was dressed in a pair of chocolate-brown slacks and a light beige blouse.

"Good morning," she said as she wheeled herself toward the coffee machine.

"Good morning," he returned. "Did you sleep well?"

"Like a baby, once I finally fell asleep," she said as she poured herself a cup of coffee and then moved to her spot at the kitchen table, her gaze not quite meeting his. "What about you?"

"It took me a long time to fall asleep, too, but once I did, I slept fine." He carried his cup to the table and sat across from her. He studied her over his cup, loving how she looked with the morning sun drifting through the window and playing on the pale strands of her hair.

"You worried me last night. You seemed to close yourself off when I asked you about your leg."

Her cheeks took on a pink hue. "Sorry. Sometimes I don't have a good handle on my emotions." She took a sip of her coffee and then finally met his gaze. "While we were in bed together, I felt so normal and so whole, and then you asked me about my leg and it just hit me that I wasn't normal or whole and never would be again."

He reached across the table and took one of her hands in his. "Melanie, I'm not sure what it will take to convince you that you are normal, that you're more whole than half the people walking around in this town."

She squeezed his hand and released it, then smiled at him gratefully. "So what are the plans for today? I'm not sure what I'm supposed to do the day after a stranger has broken into my bedroom and has tried to kill me. Is there a manual to tell me what comes next?"

"No manual, but we'll definitely want to touch base with Cameron and see what he's found out. I talked to Nick this morning and we're invited to the ranch house for lunch."

She eyed him dubiously. "That sounds like it's going to be too hard. It would require getting into your truck and loading my wheelchair, and aren't there several stairs going up to the porch of the ranch house?"

"All easily maneuvered if you just trust me," he replied.

She continued to gaze at him, her eyes windows to all the emotions shifting through her…uneasiness, a touch of fear and, finally, acceptance. "Okay, if you think you can manage it. It might be nice to meet your brother and his wife."

"And don't forget about Garrett, their almost two-year-old little terror," Adam said lightly, but he knew the depth of his love for the child was evident in his voice.

She gazed out the window, where a perfect autumn day was displayed. "It would be nice to get out of here for a little while," she admitted.

"Good. Then I'll call Nick back and tell him we'll be there around noon."

"Do you think it's safe for me to be out?" A hint of fear lingered in her eyes.

"He attacked you in your own home in the middle of the night. I think you're fine to go out and be among people. In fact, I think it's a good idea to get you out of here for the afternoon. We might even stop in at the café for dinner, let people know that you're just fine and not running scared."

"I'm definitely not running anywhere," she said as she sat up straighter in her chair. "And if this is all Craig Jenkins's doing, then I'll make sure he can't get this house even if he kills me. I'll contact my lawyer and have a will written up and leave the place to you."

Adam blinked in stunned surprise. "You can't do that, Melanie. If you're going to leave it to anyone, it should be Tilly."

Melanie shook her head. "Tilly already has a house of her own. If I leave this one to her, it would just be a financial burden on her."

"This is all a ridiculous conversation, because I have

no intention of allowing anything to happen to you!" Adam exclaimed with more force than necessary. "I don't even want to think about you worrying about having a will. You aren't about to die anytime soon. You'll have years and years to decide what you want to do with this place when the time is right."

She released a small sigh and smiled at him. "I'm beginning to think that the best thing I ever did was rent the upstairs to you."

He returned her smile. "You sure didn't seem too eager on the day I showed up on your doorstep."

Her smile faded and her gaze left his and instead once again focused outside the window. "Adam, about last night. I just want to make sure you know that it's never been in my plans or wishes to marry or have children. What happened last night won't be happening again."

His heart took a nosedive, but he nodded. "At least we're on the same page as far as marriage and children go," he replied, although he was beginning to believe his bachelorhood wasn't quite as confirmed as it had once been. "But as long as we both are on the same page, I don't see why we can't enjoy being together in bed and out."

Her gaze shot back to him and a small smile curved the corners of her mouth. "You are a naughty man, Adam Benson."

"The question is, are you a naughty woman?" he asked, his heart suddenly beating fast and furious.

"You want to see just how naughty I can be?" She

wheeled back from the table. "Follow me." She headed toward the bedroom.

Adam jumped up from the table and hurried after her, aware that if he wasn't very careful, he would be completely and totally in love with Melanie Brooks.

Mary Mathis wiped the counter in the café for the fifth time in the last twenty minutes. It was just after eight and the morning rush was in full swing.

Each time the door opened, her gaze went in that direction, seeking a face that had become achingly familiar. Every morning for the past year she'd opened the café early to allow in a single customer...Sheriff Cameron Evans.

He'd sit at the counter and cradle a cup of coffee between his big hands as they shared friendly talk. She mostly talked about the funny incidents that had happened at the café with customers or staff, or she spoke of her ten-year-old son, Matt, and all the activities and interests he had.

Cameron spoke of his job as sheriff, whatever case he was working on and about his parents, Lila and Ralph, who still lived on the family ranch just outside of Grady Gulch.

It was light, easy conversation and Mary hadn't realized how much she looked forward to it each morning until this morning, when he hadn't shown up at all.

It was just as well, she thought as she poured coffee for one of the customers and picked up an order for another. Getting close to Cameron in any way had been foolish. She knew he wanted their friendship to go to the next level. She'd begun to see a longing in his eyes when he talked to her, a longing that both drew her and repelled her.

"George, how's your breakfast?" she asked the older man who came in for nearly every meal and sat on the same stool at the counter.

"The coffee is bitter and the hash browns are too crispy," he replied gruffly.

Mary had expected nothing less. If it wasn't for complaining, George would have no conversations at all. "You want to call Rusty out and you can talk to him about the potatoes?"

"No, too late now. I've about eaten them all," George replied.

Few customers who knew the café's cook, Rusty Albright, took their complaints to him. Rusty looked more like an ex-boxer than a man who could make a great meringue, and more than once Mary had used him as a bouncer to take care of an unruly diner.

She left George and moved down the counter, her gaze sweeping over the other diners who were there enjoying breakfast. Brandon Williams sat in his motorized wheelchair, visiting with the shyer Thomas Manning. Both men had moved to town within the past year and this was the first time she'd seen Thomas talking to anyone except the waitress that served him.

She carried the coffee carafe to the end of the counter where Dennis Marrow sat, a newspaper in hand and a half a cup of coffee in front of him.

Dennis was the father of three children under the age of five. When he'd complained that mornings at the Marrow house were so chaotic he never got to read the paper in peace, his wife had offered him an hour off each morning, when he could come here for coffee and reading.

"More coffee, Dennis?" Mary asked.

The young man lowered the paper and smiled. "No thanks, Mary. I've got five minutes and then I need to get out of here and back home."

He returned to his paper as she stepped away. He never lingered, was always home on time. Their marriage would probably last at least fifty years, Mary thought. They were so young and had already learned the fine art of compromise.

Mary had once believed she'd be celebrating anniversary after anniversary, that when she'd said her vows years ago, they actually meant something. But that hadn't been in the cards for her and the choices she'd made since then would forever keep her alone, would forever keep her from reaching out for love ever again.

Still, she couldn't halt the leap of her heart when the café door opened and Cameron walked in. He looked so handsome, so tall and strong in his khaki uniform, but there was no smile on his features as he slid onto one of the empty chairs at the counter.

"You're a bit late this morning," Mary said as she poured him a cup of coffee. "I hope it's because you overslept."

"Fat chance," he replied, a deep frown cutting across his handsome forehead. "Melanie Brooks was attacked last night in her home." He kept his voice low, so Mary had to lean forward to hear him.

She gasped. "Is she all right?"

He nodded. "She's fine, but it looks like it's possible our killer isn't finished or hasn't moved on yet."

Mary was horrified by the news, but there was a tiny part of her that was relieved that the latest potential victim hadn't been a waitress from her café.

With the murders of the first two women, Mary had begun to think that somebody was targeting her personally by killing members of her staff, women she cared about.

"Any clues?" she asked.

Cameron shook his head, his frown deepening. "It was almost midnight when I got the call and we spent most of the rest of the night chasing down alibis and looking for any fingerprints or physical evidence that might have been left behind. But we didn't get the answers we needed."

"And so you're back on the merry-go-round of long hours and too little sleep," Mary replied sympathetically.

Cameron smiled at her ruefully. "And I'm not sure but I think I'm on my way to an ulcer."

"Cameron, you have to take care of yourself," Mary replied, wishing she were in a position to take care of him, to feed him properly and see that he got his rest.

But that would never happen. No matter how much she cared about Cameron, no matter how she ached to fall into his arms, to explore the emotions she sometimes saw in his eyes when he gazed at her, she would never allow that to happen. She couldn't allow that to happen.

This man, who was sworn to protect the people in Grady Gulch, the man who made her heart beat faster than any man had in the past ten years, had the capacity to destroy her life if he got too close.

By allowing him any deeper into her life, she took the risk of losing everything most dear to her...her café, her friends and, most importantly, the son who was her very life.

Chapter 12

Melanie didn't want to go to lunch at the Benson ranch, but she also didn't want to stay in the house, which no longer felt like a sanctuary.

The very last thing she wanted was to sit around with Adam and remember everything they had shared the night before and again this morning. In one sentence she had been telling him that they couldn't make love again, and before the conversation was over, she'd enticed him back into her bed. Adam was a passionate, gentle lover who had touched her not only physically, but emotionally, as well.

As she got ready for the lunch outing, she couldn't stop thinking about what it had felt like to be in his arms, to feel his naked skin against her own. It had been sheer magic...until the moment he'd asked her about her foot.

The magic had vanished and reality had slammed into her with the force of an eighteen-wheeler. Reality was that he was a temporary boarder who would eventually move on with his life and she knew in the very depths of her being that his new life wouldn't include her.

The fact that he'd worried about hurting her because of her leg, that it was the first thing he'd asked about after their beautiful lovemaking the night before made her realize that whether he would admit it or not, he hadn't forgotten even in the throes of desire that she was a woman in a wheelchair.

He hadn't made the same mistake when they'd tumbled into bed together that morning, but his concern from the night before had continued to play in her head.

As she pulled on a long-sleeved pink sweater to go with the jeans she'd already wrangled on, she also couldn't help but think about the horrific events that had happened before they made love.

If Craig Jenkins wasn't the culprit, had she been targeted as the next victim by the serial killer? Had his unsuccessful attempt only created a need to try to kill her again?

The thing that horrified her most of all was that he'd known her name, and that meant there was a strong possibility that she knew him. Was it possible that one of the male dancers she used to hang out with in New York was mentally twisted and had followed her here to Grady Gulch? The murders in the small town hadn't begun until she'd come back here. Had she brought danger home with her?

No matter how hard she racked her brain, she couldn't come up with a name of anyone she thought might be capable of murder, especially ones as senseless as these. And if somebody had followed her from New York to Grady Gulch, then why would they kill Candy Bailey and Shirley Cook? Besides, a male dancer from New York City suddenly appearing in the small town of Grady Gulch, Oklahoma, would definitely be fodder for gossip.

Looking for a killer who might have reason to want her crazy or dead could be a waste of energy. There was no way she had any connection to the other two victims. Maybe she'd just been picked randomly, an easy kill because she couldn't walk, because she couldn't run away.

She shoved these thoughts out of her head, determined to focus on more positive things, as she finished getting ready to go and meet Nick's brother, his wife and their little son.

She'd gone to high school with Nick. He was a year older than her and she had only vague memories of a dark-haired, handsome young man walking the halls. She didn't know his wife, Courtney, at all. Adam had explained to her that Courtney had grown up and gone to school in the nearby town of Evanston.

With a quick spritz of her favorite perfume she proclaimed herself ready. She wheeled into the living room, where Adam awaited her. His smile warmed her from head to toe and made her think of how his lips had felt against her own mere hours before.

"You look great," he said.

"You said casual," she said, a sudden attack of nerves

zinging through her as she slid her hands down her jean-clad legs.

"Absolutely. If we showed up in anything but jeans, Courtney and Nick wouldn't know how to treat us."

"Are you sure you can get me into their house?" she asked worriedly.

"It's not going to be a problem," he replied.

"What about getting me from my wheelchair into your truck?"

"Get that frown off your face," he demanded with mock anger. "We're not going to have any problems, okay?"

"Okay," she replied, realizing that she trusted him completely. If he said it was possible, then it was definitely so.

It took only seconds for him to wheel her out of the house and down the ramp toward the driveway, where his truck was parked.

"Oh, by the way, I arranged for a security system to be put in here while we're gone this afternoon," he announced.

She sat up straighter in her chair in alarm. Didn't he realize she couldn't afford a security system? He'd definitely overstepped the boundaries of their relationship this time. "Adam," she began.

He stopped her from saying whatever she was about to say by placing his hands on her shoulders and giving them a gentle squeeze. "I'm paying for it and it's for my own peace of mind."

She tilted her head back to look at him and he grinned.

"Hey, you aren't the only one living in that house. I

don't want some bogeyman sneaking up on me while I'm sound asleep."

"I don't think you really fit the killer's profile," she replied dryly as they came to a stop by the passenger side of his truck.

"You never know. It's possible somebody could mistake me as a girlish figure if I have enough blankets over me."

She laughed. Not in a million years would anyone ever mistake his big, strong body as a female one, even if he was covered with a hundred blankets.

Her laughter died just as quickly as it had begun as he opened the truck's passenger door. The distance from where she sat to the seat in his truck looked immense. The truck was high enough off the ground that she knew there was no way she could simply stand and carefully balance on one foot and then pivot to sit.

The old helplessness, a surge of self-pity and anger rose up inside her. She couldn't even get into a damn vehicle to take a ride without help.

"Some people can't even get out of bed," Adam said softly, as if he'd read her thoughts, as if he felt her negative emotions. "Soldiers come home from the war with no legs or no arms and yet continue to lead productive, happy lives."

His words shamed her, and she suspected he'd meant to do that. He reached down and put the brakes on her chair, then crouched down beside her. "I know this is all hard on you, Melanie, but at some point you have to realize that you're still a vital, valuable human being. You need to keep focused on the things you can do, and other than walking, I don't believe there's a thing in this world you can't do, especially after last night. Quick thinking and the ability to force yourself to move saved your life." He frowned, as if worried that he'd made her mad.

She reached out her hand and placed her palm on the side of his face. "Thanks. I needed that. Now, get me out of this chair and into your truck so we can enjoy a lunch at your family's ranch."

He stood and slid a hand beneath her knees as she wrapped her arms around his neck, and in one graceful movement he lifted her out of the chair and deposited her solidly on the truck seat. "See? That was easy."

And it had been. She buckled herself in as he wheeled the chair to the back of the truck, folded it down and then loaded it onto the bed.

Moments later they were on their way, a pleasantly warm breeze flowing through the open windows of the cab.

"We'd better enjoy this mild weather," he said as he gestured to his lowered window. "Winter will be here before long."

"Ugh, I hate winter. The cold seeps through my bones and there's nothing to do to pass the gray, snowy days," she said.

"I love winter. There's nothing better than curling up in front of a roaring fire with a cup of hot chocolate or cider in your hand. You can watch a marathon of old movies, go through a box of old pictures or just cuddle beneath an oversize fleece blanket."

She looked at him in surprise. "Who would have

guessed that the heart of a true romantic beat in that big, broad chest?" she teased.

He flashed a wry smile. "There's only a few chosen people I allow to see that particular side of me."

Melanie relaxed against the seat, her head filled with a vision of the two of them snuggled beneath a blanket with a fire crackling and popping in the living-room fireplace.

Would he still be staying in her house when the snow started falling? That would be only a month or two from now. Or would he have moved on to another location and perhaps a new woman by then?

She willed these thoughts away. It was a beautiful day and tomorrow was just a promise, and yesterday already a memory. The only thing to cling to was the present and she couldn't think of anything else she'd rather be doing than sitting next to Adam at this moment.

His clean, woodsy scent eddied in the interior of the truck cab, a scent that had filled her bedroom the night before and chased away any imagined odor of evil that might have lingered there.

As they drew closer to the ranch, Melanie felt a nervous flutter in her stomach. She told herself it didn't matter to her whether Nick and Courtney liked her or not. After all, it wasn't like they were going to be permanent fixtures in her life. Still, even knowing that, it seemed terribly important to her that they did like her.

The Benson place was a rambling ranch house guarded on either side by tall, massive evergreens that stood sentry as wind barriers. As Adam parked the truck, Melanie eyed with trepidation the three stairs that led up to the wraparound porch and front door.

She felt the nerve that pulsed in her neck as he got out of the truck and brought her the wheelchair. She was grateful that nobody was standing on the porch to watch the process of Adam lifting her from the truck to the chair and then wheeling her to the stairs, where he turned her around and pulled her backward up each step to the porch.

"Piece of cake," he said as he knocked on the door.

It had been a piece of cake. For months Melanie had worried about the logistics of leaving the house, had grieved over the fact that she would probably never be able to have lunch dates with girlfriends, that she would be a prisoner inside the house, with only Tilly's occasional company to break the monotony.

Maybe fate had blown Adam in her direction to kick her butt, to remind her that she still had a life to live and it could be lived very well from a wheelchair.

She sat up straighter as the door opened and Nick smiled in greeting. "Hey, guys. Come on in. Courtney is in the kitchen and the rug rat is running around here somewhere." He stepped back so that Adam could push Melanie across the threshold.

When Courtney appeared in the living room, Adam made the introductions all the way around.

"Melanie, why don't you come on in the kitchen with me? You can cut up some lettuce for the salad while I finish up with the chicken," Courtney said. "We'll leave the men out here to do their male bonding."

"Sounds like a plan," Melanie agreed, pleased that

Courtney had given her a task to help with the upcoming meal and wasn't treating her like a strange guest or an invalid.

She started wheeling herself across the room but halted when a darling little dark-haired toddler with a cleft chin just like Nick's raced into the room and then came to a stop at the sight of her.

"And you must be Garrett," Melanie said as she wheeled herself a little closer to where he stood.

He nodded and moved a step closer to her, his gaze sweeping not just her, but also the wheelchair curiously. With the quickness of a hummingbird he ran to her and crawled up on her lap. "Go!" he said.

Nick, Courtney and Adam froze, as if an enormous faux pas had just been committed and they weren't sure how to react to it. Melanie knew exactly how to react. With the warmth of the little boy snuggled in her arms, with his complete acceptance of who and what she was, joy filled her heart.

Together she and Garrett made the noise of a roaring car engine as she wheeled him into the kitchen.

"Have you told her yet that you're in love with her?" Nick asked Adam.

Adam turned and looked at his brother in surprise. The two were out in the stables, having left the women and Garrett alone in the house after lunch.

Adam started to protest, but then he stuck his hands in his pockets of his jacket and sighed. "Is it that obvious?"

"Maybe only to me," Nick said with a small smile.

"But I've never seen you look at a woman the way you look at her. It's the same way I look at Courtney." Nick stroked the mane of one of the horses in the stalls. "You know how she feels about you?"

Adam toyed with the plastic chips in his pocket. "I never thought much about having a wife and kids. And according to Melanie, she has no intention of ever getting married or having a family."

Nick grinned at him as they moved farther down the building, which smelled of fresh hay, leather and horse. "You know how that goes. You tell yourself that until you find the right one, and then you can't wait to get a ring on her finger. You can't wait to spend as much of each day as you can with her and have her in your bed next to you every single night."

"That's what I want with Melanie," Adam said, vaguely surprised to recognize his want, even more surprised to verbalize it. The fear that somehow he'd turn into a Sam had vanished in the moments he'd spoken to his brother that morning on the phone.

There was no question that Sam had mental issues, but Adam had recognized there was no hidden mental illness inside himself. Was he ready to admit that he wanted, needed, a family of his own? He'd never wanted that before, but Melanie made him want those things.

They left the stables but stood just outside the door, with the warm afternoon sunshine on their shoulders.

"Have you really thought it through? I mean, what it would require to be married to a woman in a wheelchair?" Nick asked.

"Probably not," Adam admitted. "But it doesn't

matter to me. Whenever I'm with her, I don't see the wheelchair. I see only her. I know she'll need help occasionally, but she's fiercely independent and I don't care what extra care might be required."

"Just make sure that if you decide to pursue it, it's with your eyes wide open."

"I think they are," Adam replied and then frowned. "I'm just not sure that she feels the same way about me. I know she likes me." He thought of their lovemaking and felt a warmth sweep into his cheeks. But lots of women these days fell into bed with men fairly easily, with no intention of following through on a real relationship. Still, he couldn't believe that Melanie was one of those women. Surely she had to care about him more than just a little.

Nick clapped him on the shoulder. "Good luck with things, with her. I'd love to see you settled down and happy with a family of your own. There's nothing like it. And now we'd better head back to the house."

As they walked, Adam checked his watch. "I was hoping that I would have heard something from Cameron by now." He'd told Nick and Courtney about the attack on Melanie and the fact that a security system was being installed while they were eating lunch.

"Maybe he doesn't have anything to report," Nick replied.

"He should have at least checked out some alibis by now." They halted at the foot of the porch.

"Like whose?" Nick asked curiously.

Adam frowned thoughtfully. "Melanie gave him a couple of names of people she was seeing years ago, before she left town. Denver Walton, Jim Collins and Billy Vickers were three people he should have checked out."

"Those are surely dead ends. Denver was probably in bed with Maddy, Jim was on duty and Billy Vickers was probably sleeping with his new wife." It was Nick's turn to frown. "You know, now that I think about it, Billy Vickers's wife looks a lot like Melanie. She's got the same blond hair and pretty features."

Adam thought about Linda Vickers, née Cochran. She did bear a close resemblance to Melanie, but did that mean anything? She and Billy had married about six months before and appeared to be deliriously happy together.

Adam had a feeling there was nothing to report because there wasn't a real, viable trail to follow. It seemed crazy to consider that somebody from ten years ago might have a personal beef with Melanie. It was more likely she'd been attacked by the serial killer who had murdered the two women in town, and so far Cameron had no clues to point to the identity of that person.

"I heard you talked to Sam," Nick said. "He called me just after he spoke to you."

Adam nodded, thinking of the early morning call he'd gotten while Melanie was still in bed, asleep. "I think he was shocked when I actually answered his call."

"How did it go?"

Adam thought of the brief conversation he'd had with his eldest brother. "Fine, I guess. He seemed happy to talk to me but there's no question he's still ill. He was fine for a few minutes and then began a rant on how it wasn't fair that anyone was happy when he was so miserable, that he wanted to hurt all the happy people in the world. He's a different man. The Sam, the brother I knew and loved, is gone."

Nick clapped him on the shoulder. "I know, but maybe once his trial is over, somebody will see to it that he gets some treatment. He'll never be the same, but maybe some medication or therapy will help him find some peace inside himself."

Adam nodded and fought off a wave of discouragement as they reentered the house. His heart instantly lifted as he heard the sounds of laughter coming from the kitchen.

Nick and Adam entered that room to find Courtney and Melanie seated at the table and Garrett in Melanie's lap, both his mouth and Melanie's smeared with the icing from a piece of chocolate cake.

He'd take a bite and then turn to feed Melanie a bite. "Melly cake," he said proudly to the two men.

Melanie laughed and quickly grabbed a napkin. She wiped her face and then Garrett's. "He won't let me feed myself."

"He's taken quite a shine to Melanie!" Courtney exclaimed.

"I think it's the wheels. You know how men are when it comes to a good set of wheels," Melanie replied with another laugh.

Garrett nodded, as if he understood exactly what she was talking about, and everyone laughed. It was a great way to end their time together and within another half an hour Melanie and Adam were back in his truck and headed home.

Adam's heart was filled with the vision of Garrett and Melanie together. He had watched her interact with the little boy and had envisioned her with his child. She would be beautiful pregnant and would make such a loving mother.

"You were good with Garrett," he said as they pulled onto the road that would lead them back to Main Street.

"He's a real cutie."

"I think you'd make a terrific mom." He shot her a quick glance and caught a look of grief that stole across her features in a flash and then disappeared.

"It's just not in the cards for me," she replied, her voice calm despite what he had just seen on her face.

"But you could have children if you wanted to." He wasn't sure why he was pressing the issue.

"Physically yes, I'm capable of having children, but I decided a long time ago that motherhood wasn't for me, and going into a wheelchair certainly hasn't changed my mind."

"Too bad," Adam said.

"Yeah, too bad for me."

He glanced at her again and then back at the road. "No, I was thinking too bad for the children who will miss out on being loved by you."

She turned her head and stared out the window and didn't speak again until they pulled up in front of the house. "I guess the security system has been installed?" she asked as he lifted her from the passenger seat and placed her in her wheelchair.

"The code is my birthday." He smiled. "I didn't know yours, so I figured I'd tell them to make it mine." He gave her the numbers as he pushed her up the ramp to the front door. "Every door and window is covered, so nobody will be sneaking into the house again without us knowing about it."

"I'll definitely sleep easier at night." She unlocked the door and pushed it open and instantly a warning beep sounded. The control panel was set in the foyer and she wheeled over to it and punched in the number to turn the system off.

Adam showed her how to reset it. "It should be activated at all times. A security system works only if it's on."

"Got it," she replied.

They talked about going to the café for dinner but decided to just stay in. They had a quiet dinner and it was later in the evening when Adam came downstairs for a can of soda and found her seated at the table, a sketch pad in front of her.

"What are you working on?" he asked curiously, suddenly aware of the utter silence of the house around them.

"Silliness," she replied.

"What kind of silliness?" He grabbed a soda from the fridge and joined her at the table.

She had her hand splayed across the page, as if to hide whatever it was that was on it. She hesitated a moment and then moved her hand aside.

He looked with interest at the drawing of some sort

of frilly thing on the page. "What is it?" he asked curiously.

"A dance costume." She felt the warmth of a blush color her cheeks. "I've been sketching them since I first started to dance. These are my fantasy costumes, the ones I would have used for recitals if I was going to have a dance studio of my own."

"May I?" He gestured toward the sketch pad.

Once again she hesitated. It was like showing him a piece of her dreams, a personal part of herself she'd never shown anyone else. Not even Tilly or her mother had seen all the sketches she'd done over the years. With a tremulous breath she shoved the thick book toward him and held her breath as he began to turn the pages.

"I'm not a dancer, but these look incredibly creative," he finally said.

Once again her cheeks warmed, this time with pleasure. "I see them in my mind and I know exactly what kind of material each is made of, where to place the specialty decorations and still keep the costume light and moveable."

He pushed the sketch pad back in front of her, his eyes lit with a shine that for some reason shot a tiny wave of excitement through her. "Does Tilly know how to sew?" he asked.

"Sure, and so do I. I learned in sixth grade from my mother. We made lots of my costumes when I was assigned solo dances."

"Maybe this is your future, Melanie." He leaned forward across the table, his eyes warm and filled with a simmering anticipation. "You could put up a website.

You have all the credentials you need, and with your sewing skills you could probably make a fortune selling these things to dancers around the country."

For a moment the hope that sparked in his eyes also heated her heart. Was this what she was supposed to do? Certainly she had spent years drawing the kinds of costumes she'd want to wear as a dancer. While her sewing skills might be rusty, she was sure that spending a little time with a sewing machine would sharpen those skills once again.

The hope lasted for only a moment and then the taste of failure filled her mouth. "Adam, it would be a nice plan, but it's not something I can do right now."

"Why not?" he asked. "I could see by the way your eyes just lit up that you were excited. What's standing in your way?" She didn't reply, but it was as if he could suddenly see inside her head. "I'll back you, Melanie. I'll provide the seed money you'd need to get started."

"I could never ask you to do that," she protested as she closed the sketch pad.

"You didn't ask, I offered. Besides, it would be a business deal and I'd expect you to pay me back once you became profitable."

Melanie felt the burn of tears in her eyes as hope once again buoyed up inside her. Could she really do this? Could she build a financial future for herself based on a book full of drawings and her knowledge as a dancer? The answer was yes. She believed in her heart, in her very soul, that this could work.

"I think maybe you just gave me a new dream," she finally said.

"Then while I'm on your good side, I'd like to ask you a question," he said.

"What's that?" she asked, her heart lighter than it had felt in months.

"Why don't you allow any music in your life?"

She leaned back in her chair and gazed at him thoughtfully, wondering if there was any way she could make him understand what music did to her.

"I feel it in my heart, in the very depths of my soul," she began. "I've never been able to understand how people can listen to music and not move, not at least tap their feet or drum their fingers on a tabletop to the rhythm. When I hear it, it sings in my veins, making it impossible for me to sit still. And now, since I can't dance, the sound of music is just torture to me."

The mourning that swept through her was like what she might have felt for an old friend who'd passed away several years ago. She recognized at that moment that she was moving into an acceptance stage, which she hoped would eventually become a complete healing.

"Music should never be torture," Adam protested. He frowned thoughtfully. "We definitely need to do something to change that."

Before she could guess his intent, he got up and grabbed the handles of her wheelchair. "What…what are you doing?" she asked as he wheeled her into the living room.

He stopped when they reached the middle of the room. He walked around in front of her and crouched down so that they were eye to eye. "Do you trust me, Melanie?" he asked.

"Of course," she said without hesitation. Somehow, someway in the last couple of weeks she'd come to trust Adam as she hadn't trusted anyone in a long time, but as he walked over to the stereo system on the shelving unit against one wall, she tensed.

"Adam, please…don't."

He turned back to look at her once again. "Do you trust me, Melanie?" he asked again.

She knew what he was about to do and her heart hammered an unsteady beat. It was going to hurt. He was going to force her to listen to music in some misguided effort to help her. Yet even knowing that this was going to be a form of exquisite torture, she nodded once again to answer his question.

She knew the radio was tuned to a classical station, and when he punched the on button, the strains of Tchaikovsky filled the room.

Her heart swelled with the familiar music and the beats resounded in the blood that flowed through her veins. She wanted to rise up from her chair and whirl around the room. She wanted to lose herself in the very magic of dance. Instead she tightened her hands on her wheelchair armrests and fought back a wave of tears.

Once again Adam crouched down in front of her. "You can still dance, Melanie," he said softly. "You can move your arms. You can move your body to the rhythm while you sit in that chair. You can close your eyes and dance all you want in your mind, or you can dance with me."

Before she recognized his intent, he scooped her

up into his arms. "I've got you, Melanie. Now dance for me."

At first she wasn't sure what he meant. How could she dance while she was held in his arms? What was he doing to her? Why was he doing this to her?

She closed her eyes against new hot tears, but as the music continued to play and her heart opened to it, allowed it inside her, she instinctively raised her arms over her head and began to sway and dance to the music.

She arched her back, arms still thrown over her head, and trusted that Adam would keep her safe, as she'd trusted so many other male dance partners over the years.

Lost, she became lost in movement and rhythm, and although she couldn't really *dance* with her bad leg and foot, every other part of her body interpreted the music with joy.

She didn't imagine that she was onstage. She was content knowing that she was in Adam's arms, dancing with him. She no longer needed the stage lights to make her feel special. He made her feel special.

It was only when the song ended that she opened her eyes and released a tremulous sigh of happiness.

"That was beautiful," Adam said hoarsely as he tightened his grip on her.

She stared at him, this handsome cowboy who had invaded her house, invaded her life. The man who had restored her laughter, had shown her that she could still have a life and, most importantly of all, had brought back her music and her dance. Certainly those things weren't the same, would never be the same again. But Adam had shown her that she could have some of it back, that she could still enjoy it.

It was at that moment she realized that despite her every intention to the contrary, she was in love with Adam Benson. It was also at that moment that his cell phone rang.

He carefully deposited her back into her wheelchair and then dug his cell phone out of his pocket. He looked at the caller identification and then at her.

"It's Cameron," he said and just that quickly the magic of dance, the wonder of Adam disappeared as she thought of the man who had crept into her room in the middle of the night, the man who apparently wanted her dead.

Chapter 13

Cameron sat across the table from Adam and Melanie, his features giving them all the answers they needed. Nothing. He had absolutely nothing for them. It was evident in the defeat that darkened his eyes, in the exhaustion that wearied his features. Adam fought the bitterness of disappointment, which threatened to crawl up the back of his throat.

"Since last night we've focused our investigation mainly on the possibility that the attack on you might have been a personal one and not tied to the other two murders," Cameron said to them.

Adam nodded. He understood that it would be easier to approach the investigation that way initially to rule out any of the people who might have a personal beef against Melanie. "So what have you got so far?"

"At the time of the attack Billy Vickers was in bed with his wife. Of course she confirmed it. He appeared genuinely surprised to find out that you were back here in town. He said he'd just assumed after your mother's death you'd gone back to New York City."

"So he's off the suspect list," Melanie said.

"Not quite. While I was speaking with Billy and Linda in the living room, Deputy Temple asked to use the restroom, where he did a little snooping in the medicine cabinet and discovered a prescription bottle for some fairly heavy-duty sleeping pills for Linda."

"Then it's possible Billy slipped his wife a pill before bedtime and she wouldn't have known for sure if he left their bedroom in the middle of the night or not," Adam said.

Cameron nodded. "Exactly."

"But I haven't even seen Billy since I left here for New York years ago," Melanie said.

Adam frowned. "I think he and his wife might have been at the Cowboy Café the night we went."

"He didn't stop by the table to say hello or anything," Melanie replied. "I didn't notice him there."

"If he was with his wife, then he probably wouldn't have stopped by to say hello to an old girlfriend." Adam shrugged.

"We weren't boyfriend and girlfriend. We just dated a couple of times, that's all," Melanie said, as if needing to explain her relationship with Billy.

"In any case, Denver Walton and Maddy were together at the Corral until well after midnight and there were plenty of witnesses to corroborate their story."

The Corral was a hot spot for drinking and dancing at the edge of town. For a couple of months after Sam's arrest Adam had spent more than his share of time there, doing very little dancing but a lot of drinking.

"And of course, Jim Collins was on duty," Cameron continued, "which brings us to Craig Jenkins. I've been unable to locate him to check out his alibi. He hasn't been home all day and I was finally able to contact his secretary this afternoon and she told me he left yesterday morning to go out of town."

"Out of town where?" Melanie asked.

"She didn't know. He's supposed to be back in a couple of days and hopefully we'll get some answers from him then."

Adam frowned. He didn't like loose ends and Craig Jenkins was definitely a loose end at this point in time. As far as Adam was concerned, Craig had the most to gain by Melanie's death. How simple it would be to kill her and make it look like the work of the serial killer.

"Kevin Naperson was at home with his parents last night. Of course, they probably wouldn't have known if he'd sneaked out of his room in the middle of the night, so he's not been crossed off the list." Cameron looked at Melanie. "Have you thought of anyone else you think we should check out?"

She sighed and shook her head. "No, and trust me, I've racked my brain. The only reason why this attack felt personal was that he knew my name, but he could know my name and still be the serial killer working here in town."

"I know," Cameron replied curtly.

"If it is the same person who killed Shirley and Candy, have you been able to figure out at all why he's killing these women? What motivates him?" Adam asked.

Cameron raked his fingers through his hair and shook his head. "We know the murders don't appear to be sexually motivated. The victims aren't molested and there are no elements that would point to a sexual motivation."

"I've heard it said that there are only three motives for murder. Sex, greed and revenge," Adam said. "Is there any way greed or revenge could be pointed to as a motive in the cases of Candy Bailey and Shirley Cook?" he asked.

"Not that we've been able to find." Cameron leaned back in the chair. "And there's one other motive for murder besides the three you named."

"What's that?" Adam asked.

"Some murderers kill just because they like it and that's what I'm afraid we're dealing with here," Cameron said. "A thrill killer. They are often the most difficult ones to catch."

Adam could almost feel the icy chill that swept through Melanie. He reached beneath the table and took her cold hand in his. "But you will catch him," he said to Cameron.

Cameron's eyes narrowed. "Eventually his need to kill will overcome his control and hopefully he'll start making mistakes. He'll begin to decompensate, get sloppy or take risks, and we can only hope that will happen soon."

"And in the meantime?" Melanie asked with a squeeze of Adam's hand.

"And in the meantime I see you've had a security system installed. That's smart, because if this is the same guy who killed Candy and Shirley, then he likes the nighttime and he likes going in places where there's little resistance." Cameron leaned forward. "I'm holding a news conference tomorrow and reminding people to keep their doors and windows locked up. I'm going to tell the women of this town not to be out after dark alone. I'd hoped whoever was responsible for Candy's and Shirley's murders had left town or died or got arrested. I'd hoped his little reign of terror was over, but with this latest attack on you I have to assume that he's still active."

"If he tries to get to Melanie again, he'll not only have to somehow get through the security system, but he'll also have to come through me," Adam said fervently.

Cameron nodded and wearily rose to his feet. "I'm guessing that he'll go after somebody else, that he'll recognize that Melanie is no longer a vulnerable victim, but there are certainly no guarantees. We still can't be sure we're dealing with the same perp."

Adam stood, as well, wishing that Cameron had brought some sort of closure with him. "You'll stay in touch?" he asked as he walked the lawman to the front door. "I'll be particularly interested in finding out where Craig Jenkins disappeared to."

"I'd like to know where he disappeared to, also,"

Cameron replied. "I find it damned suspicious that Melanie is attacked and Craig suddenly disappears."

"And if he's behind this, I definitely know his motivation," Adam added. "Greed. We both know this house is prime real estate for commercial buildings. Melanie told me that her mother owes some back taxes, which she'd been paying off. If she's killed, then the house would probably go up for auction for the back taxes. Jenkins would be able to pick it up for a song."

"All the more reason for me to talk to him," Cameron said, with a deep frown cutting across his forehead. "I've got some deputies in Evanston watching his house for his return. He'll be brought in for questioning the minute he makes an appearance."

"And if he doesn't show up?" Adam asked.

"Then we'll go hunting until we find him." The two men stopped at the front door. "How is she handling things?" Cameron gestured back toward the kitchen.

"She's amazingly strong." The pride that swelled up in Adam's chest felt like his own. He was proud of her, of how well she'd handled what might have broken most women. "We both had a few minutes of concern when we thought she had broken those pictures in the living room, but there's no doubt in my mind that whoever attacked her also gained access to the house and broke the glass in an effort to torment her."

"She's been tormented enough. Now we need some answers," Cameron replied intently. With that the two men said their goodbyes.

Once Cameron left, Adam reset the alarm system and then saw that Melanie had moved to the sofa in the living room. He sat down next to her. "Are you all right?" he asked.

"I'm fine." She worried a hand through her silky hair. "It would have been nice if Cameron had been able to tell me that he'd caught the bad guy and now had him in jail, but I didn't really expect that to happen."

"The important thing is that he will catch the bad guy sooner or later." Adam fought the impulse to pull her into his embrace, to bury his nose in the vanilla scent of her hair.

"Two women dead and a near miss on me. I'd say at the moment the bad guy is winning."

"Hopefully sooner than later that all will change," Adam said. As a silence fell between them, Adam remembered what it had been like to hold her in his arms while she danced to the music.

It had been magical. It was as if he'd been the jewelry box that held the ballerina in place while she whirled and twirled in graceful motion. It had been the most sensual thing he'd ever been a part of, watching her lose herself to the music, trusting him to hold her steady.

As he remembered her playing with Garrett, delighting the child as he had her, Adam couldn't stand it any longer. He needed to touch her.

He reached out for her hand, but she didn't place hers in his. Instead she appeared to draw into herself as she gazed at him. "It's been a long day." Her gaze held his for a long moment and then slid just past his shoulder. "Since you've installed the security system, I don't see any reason for you to sleep down here anymore."

Adam stared at her and waited for her gaze to finally

meet his again. This was definitely a consequence of the security system that he hadn't counted on.

He had thought they were building something together, but obviously he'd been wrong. He was preciously close to being completely in love with her, but it was obvious she didn't feel the same way.

When her gaze finally met his, he saw a distance in her eyes that broke his heart, a distance that made him feel like something had finished before it had ever really had a chance to begin.

It had been four nights since he'd gotten into Melanie Brooks's bedroom, since he'd smelled the scent of her, been so achingly close to taking her.

He wrapped his arms around himself. At two in the morning in October the air definitely was chilly. He had a feeling they were in for an early, harsh winter. Just tonight the weatherman had spoken of a cold front moving in. Melanie Brooks wouldn't live to endure the winter.

It had been fun to play with her, to get into the house and move her things and erase the caller ID. He knew it had to have screwed with her mind, but he hadn't gotten the enjoyment of seeing the fear in her eyes, of watching the horror of her believing she was going crazy. Yes, it had been fun, but now he was tired of the fun.

Five more minutes. If he'd just had five more minutes, he would have managed to get into that closet. He would have been able to drug her, then take her to his place and enjoy some "quality" time with her.

He wanted that. He wanted to see her crawl to him.

He wanted to see the fear in her eyes before he stole the life from her.

If only Adam Benson had been five minutes later getting home. Then the rage that burned inside him would have been satisfied. Melanie would be dead and he would finally be at peace.

He stared at the darkened windows of the room where he knew she slept. "Soon," he whispered as he backed out of her yard. Soon he would make a move on her again, and this time there would be no cowboy to ride to her rescue, no knight in shining armor to save the beautiful princess. She would be his and his alone to do with what he wanted.

And he wanted her dead.

Melanie sat at the kitchen table, sipping a cup of coffee. Dawn was just beginning to break over the horizon and Adam had yet to make an appearance for the day.

It had been five long days since the security system had been installed, five long days since she'd made it clear to Adam that any further intimacy between the two of them wasn't going to happen.

They had returned to a strained politeness that felt like torture to her, but it was a necessary torture. The minute she'd realized she was falling hopelessly in love with him, she'd known it was necessary to retreat. She had to protect herself. She had to protect her heart.

He'd brought so many things into her life. He'd proven to her that she could have a social life, that she could leave this house and enjoy music once again. He'd brought back her laughter and a vision for a future. And there were times in the past five days that she'd wondered if perhaps her love for him was really a case of deep gratitude.

Still, no matter how she worked to make her feelings toward him be gratefulness alone, she couldn't. It was simply love…love for him as a man, as an uncle, love for the person he was and the way he made her feel whenever he looked at her with those beautiful blue eyes of his.

She'd needed to back off not just for her own sake but, more importantly, for his. She sensed that he had a depth of feelings for her, too. And she couldn't allow that. She couldn't allow him to fall in love with her. That particular scenario had heartbreak written all over it.

Taking a sip of her coffee, she watched as the sun made its first bold peek over the last of the lingering night clouds. There hadn't been a minute that had gone by in the last five days that she hadn't wanted to be in his arms, that she hadn't wanted him to be next to her in her bed.

She felt like Juliet, but instead of it being family holding her back from reaching out for love, it was her own disability. No way would she saddle Adam with it, with her.

He deserved much more than she would ever be able to give him. He deserved a whole woman who could be an active mother to his children. And he needed children. As she'd watched him interact with his nephew, she'd seen the kind of father he would make. He was meant to be a husband and a father, just not with her.

As if he'd been summoned by her thoughts, she heard the sound of his footsteps coming down the stairs and steeled herself for another tense day.

He hadn't left the house in the past five days, and she had spent too much of her time in her bedroom, on the computer, surfing mindlessly to pass the time and keep away from him.

She wasn't sure how he'd passed each day; she knew only that his presence had been constant. There had been no more news about the attack on her and she could only assume that Adam had stayed close to the house in an effort to keep her safe.

But she felt perfectly comfortable with the security system now in place and decided that today she'd encourage him to get out, to go visit his brother and do something more constructive than hanging around here and babysitting her.

Still, when he appeared in the kitchen, freshly showered and achingly handsome, she selfishly wanted to keep him in the house with her, where she could smell the familiar scent of him and see the shine of his blue eyes whenever she wanted.

"Good morning," he said as he walked over to the counter to get himself a cup of coffee.

"Back at you," she replied.

"You're up early this morning." He slid into the chair across the table from her, his hands cupping his mug.

"I woke up early and tried to go back to sleep, but it wasn't happening, so I just decided to go ahead and get up." She gestured out the window. "The sunrise this morning is absolutely spectacular."

She watched him as he stared out the window and nodded. Each and every one of his features was indelibly burned into her brain. The slight curl of his dark hair, the straight nose and strong jawline, even the curve of his lips were more than a simple memory to her. She knew that when he decided to move on, it would take a very long time for her to forget him.

He would be her last lover. He would be the man she'd always hold in her heart to warm the cold loneliness that would accompany her through the rest of her days. Oh, there would be girlfriends to lunch with, to enjoy for conversation and friendship. Already in the last week two of her old friends from high school had called her just to chat.

But she would never again venture into the world of intimacy with a man. The risk was too high. Emotions could flare out of control, and if she did weaken and get married, she feared the man who bound himself to her would eventually only come to resent her and her special needs.

When he turned back to look at her, she quickly glanced down into her half-empty cup, afraid that he might see the love she felt for him shining in her eyes.

"You know, it isn't necessary for you to hang around here every hour of every day," she said, not looking up at him. "I feel perfectly safe here now that the security system is in place."

"Actually, I was thinking maybe you'd like to go with me to the café for breakfast this morning," he said.

She finally gazed at him, ready to tell him no, that it

wasn't a good idea for them to socialize together anymore. "Adam," she began.

He held up a hand, as if to stop her from saying whatever she intended to say. "As friends, Melanie, just landlord and tenant enjoying a meal together. Nothing more, nothing less. We've been cooped up in this house for too long and I think we both could use an outing."

She hesitated a moment and then finally nodded. She could definitely use an outing and maybe throughout the course of the meal she could figure out a way to return to the landlord-tenant relationship she'd initially intended for them to have.

"Good, and then after breakfast maybe I'll drop you back here and then I'll contact Ben Temple and see if he wants to meet me out at the shooting range." There was a hesitation in his voice, as if he was just waiting for her to tell him not to leave.

"I think that sounds like a terrific idea," she replied, both relieved and somehow disappointed that he was going to be away from the house, away from her.

You can't have it both ways, a little voice whispered inside her head. She had to let him go. She needed to gain some appropriate distance from him, both physically and emotionally. And she'd do that…right after she had breakfast with him at the café.

It was just after eight when they left her house, deciding to walk despite the brisk morning air. Adam had on his black jacket and Melanie had thrown on her navy winter coat to make the trek down the sidewalk.

She wheeled herself and Adam walked beside her and she knew this was the last time she'd have a meal with him at the café. The boundaries between them had become impossibly blurred and she needed to get them more firmly drawn once again.

It felt far too right for him to be walking beside her. It had felt far too right being held in his arms, laughing with him over silly things and making love with him.

She'd already decided he would no longer be her lover. What she had to do now was make sure she didn't lose him as a tenant. As painful as it was going to be to have him in the house, to smell his scent every day and see his smiles, his frowns and everything in between, she had to remember that this was ultimately a business deal. His rent money was all that was standing between her and Craig Jenkins owning her home.

Chapter 14

Adam drew in a lungful of the bracing morning air and tried to ignore how the sun sparkled in Melanie's hair and how her fragrance seemed to ride the slight breeze.

The past five days had been agony. Being in the same space with Melanie and yet feeling the chasm between them had been a particular kind of torture for him.

There was no question that things had changed since the night they'd danced together. It was as if she'd tuned out, turned off, and he didn't know why.

He'd realized that his feelings for her were obviously not reciprocated, but that hadn't stopped him from feeling. He'd tried to keep busy. He'd set up his computer and signed up for the classes he wanted to take, but they didn't begin until January.

He'd spoken to Cameron several times during the past five days, checking to see if there had been any progress made on the investigation into the attack on Melanie, but Cameron had nothing to report.

He'd tried to respect the fact that Melanie obviously didn't want him, that she was determined to keep herself isolated from him both emotionally and physically, but this morning he couldn't stand it. He just wanted some time with her, some quality time together, and he knew the only way to get that was to get her out of the house.

"It's going to be another beautiful day," Melanie said, pulling him from his depressing thoughts. "I thought it was supposed to turn colder."

"That's what the forecast says, but let's hope it stays nice. If this keeps up, there's going to be a lot of happy trick-or-treaters this Friday night," he replied. He smiled at her, wanting, needing, to connect. "If you were going to go trick-or-treating, what would your costume be?"

"An ugly old witch," she replied without hesitation.

He looked at her in astonishment. "Really? I would have guessed you for a swan or a princess."

"No way. I'd let my evil twin come out to play and go as a witch. What about you?"

"A sheriff, of course," he replied without thought.

"Of course," she echoed.

By that time they'd reached the café, which, as usual, was bustling with breakfast diners. Adam found them a table that was easily accessible for Melanie's wheelchair and they settled in.

"Is that Junior Lempke?" Melanie asked as she nodded in the direction of a big man clearing a table.

"It is. Mary took him under her wing a couple of years ago and put him to work. He not only buses tables, but he's also been doing some of the cooking."

"That's nice," Melanie replied and smiled as the mentally challenged young man caught sight of her and gave her a shy nod and a quick grin.

At that moment a waitress with the name tag of Lynette stopped by to take their order, and as soon as she left, Brandon Williams scooted his way toward them.

"I see a new, beautiful woman in my sights and I must come over to meet her." He smiled at Melanie and then looked at Adam expectedly.

Adam made the proper introductions between the two and for a few minutes the big man in the power scooter visited with them. Adam always enjoyed conversations with Brandon, who seemed well-educated and never shy to voice his opinion about anything.

They had just finished a rousing discussion about the merits of Halloween when Lynette appeared with their orders and Brandon returned to his own table.

"He seems nice," Melanie said.

"He's the man I told you about. He gets all over town in that motorized scooter. Maybe you need to check into getting one of those for yourself."

"Maybe I will," she agreed. "Now that I have the ramp, a motorized scooter would definitely allow me to go farther away from the house without getting tired."

As they ate their meals, they small talked about the people in the café that Melanie didn't recognize and

Adam tried his best not to get distracted by how much he wanted to kiss her again, and fought the desire to fall into the depths of her beautiful blue eyes.

"There's Kevin Naperson," he said when the young man entered the restaurant.

"He seems too skinny to have been the man in my room," Melanie said thoughtfully as she watched Kevin take a table in a corner by himself. "Of course, when I realized somebody was in my room, he became the size of a monster."

Adam looked over at Kevin. "If he's innocent in everything, then I feel sorry for him. He's basically become an outcast since Candy's murder."

"But Cameron questioned a lot of people at that time, right?"

Adam nodded. "I guess Kevin has just made a good target for everyone to distrust since then. I think at the moment everyone in town is on Cameron's list… and speak of the devil," he said as the lawman walked through the door.

Cameron went to the counter, sat on a stool and then turned around to survey the crowd. As his gaze fell on Adam and Melanie, he got up off the stool and headed toward them.

"Melanie, Adam, mind if I join you for a minute?" he asked when he reached their table. "I was going to head over to your place after I had my breakfast."

"You have news?" Melanie asked eagerly.

"Unfortunately not enough," Cameron replied, stealing away Melanie's anticipation. "Craig Jenkins has finally surfaced. I drove to Evanston last night to talk to him. His alibi is that he drove to Tulsa on the afternoon of the night of your attack. Apparently he had a big deal working for a couple of strip malls and also has relatives there, so he decided to combine business with pleasure. This morning I intend to check out the places he says he was and the people he was with to make sure his alibi is solid."

"So no news is just no news," Melanie said with obvious disappointment.

"Basically," Cameron admitted. He released a deep, weary sigh. "And that's been the story of this entire investigation." He stood. "I'll keep you posted as to what else I might find out."

"Thanks, Cameron," Adam said.

"He looks so tired," Melanie said as Cameron returned to the counter.

"These murders have kicked the stuffing out of him." Adam frowned. "I wish I could do something to help."

"Your time will come, Adam. Have you signed up for those classes you wanted to take?"

He nodded. "And I don't think I've mentioned to you that I finally talked to Sam. It took me a while to process my feelings."

"How was it?" she asked as she picked up a piece of her toast.

"Difficult, but also freeing."

She looked at him curiously. "Freeing how?"

He stabbed a piece of scrambled egg with his fork but didn't pull it up to his mouth. "When Sam was first arrested, my initial feelings were of guilt, that somehow

I hadn't seen the signs that he was mentally in trouble, that I'd let him down somehow."

"Adam, you aren't a trained mental health professional. It wasn't your job to see the signs," Melanie said softly.

He flashed her a quick smile. "I know that now, but then I started worrying that whatever mental illness Sam had might be lying dormant inside me. I started to wonder if maybe I was capable of hurting somebody… of killing somebody."

"Oh, Adam, how could you even think such a thing?" Melanie reached across the table and touched the back of his hand. "You are one of the most solid and kind men I've ever known in my life. I've seen your soul, Adam, and it's beautiful. There's nothing dark inside you, trust me."

"I'm in love with you." The words fell from his mouth on a wave of pure, spontaneous emotion.

She dropped her piece of toast and stared at him and he wasn't sure who was more shocked, Melanie or him. He hadn't meant to tell her how he felt, and even if he had planned to say the words eventually, it certainly wouldn't have been in the middle of a morning rush at the Cowboy Café.

But now that he'd said it, he was in all the way, his heart beating so fast he felt slightly faint. "I love you, Melanie."

"Stop," she hissed, her eyes darkening with an emotion he couldn't read. Fear? Anger? Regret? Worst of all, horror?

"Why should I stop?"

"Because I don't want to hear it." She stared down at her plate and picked up her fork and then set it down again and looked at him. "Because it isn't true. You just think it is. We've somehow got everything all tangled up, that's all. We crossed over the line and now things are all muddied."

"I don't feel muddied at all," he protested. "I feel very clearheaded for the first time in a very long time."

She balled up her napkin and placed it next to her plate. "Please don't say anything else. Maybe you think I need a hero and you want to be that man because you have nothing better to do at this moment in your life."

"That's the most ridiculous thing I've ever heard!" Adam exclaimed, then realized his voice had been louder than he'd intended. He leaned forward in his chair, his heart simmering with the emotion he felt for her.

"It's not so ridiculous," she countered. "You moved into my place because you were in transition. Now you've realized your ultimate goal is to become a deputy. It won't be long before you realize that goal, either here in Grady Gulch or in some other town, and then you'll realize that your feelings for me were temporary."

"How nice of you to have my life all figured out for me," Adam said with a rise of irritation. "It must be wonderful to have the special gift of looking into somebody's heart and knowing exactly what they're feeling," he added with a touch of sarcasm.

He drew a deep breath, wanting, needing, to get himself back under control. Proclaiming your love for a woman wasn't supposed to make you aggravated at her.

"Melanie," he said softly. "Would it be so terrible if I am in love with you?"

"Yes, it would be terrible." Tears shone in her eyes and she picked up her napkin, as if afraid that at any moment she might need to swipe them away. "I need you as a tenant, Adam."

He frowned in confusion. "That wouldn't change by me loving you. There has to be something else. Why are you so upset? Granted, this wasn't the best way or the best place for me to tell you how I feel, but I didn't think it would make you cry."

The tears that had threatened at her eyes fulfilled their promise and began to trek down her cheeks. "Oh, Adam." She looked down at her half-empty plate. "I don't want you to love me, because I don't love you back."

Of all the things she might have said, these were the words he hadn't expected at all. In some part of the back of his brain he'd thought she was falling for him as deeply, as profoundly, as he had fallen for her.

Her words sliced through him like a sword, and for a moment he felt headless, boneless with a killing grief. It was at that moment he realized how deep his fantasies had played out in his mind where she was concerned.

He'd been able to see them living together as husband and wife. He'd dreamed of being a deputy while he supported her business of selling costumes. He'd seen her as his wife, as the mother of his children, as his partner through life.

For a long moment he was breathless, speechless with loss, but when he realized how upset she was and that they were drawing attention to their table, he forced a smile.

"Don't be sad, Melanie. It's okay. We're okay." He picked up his fork to finish his meal and wondered how he was going to maintain his sanity living with her, loving her and yet knowing she apparently didn't love him back.

It wasn't long after Adam's declaration of love that they finished picking at their meals and then left the restaurant. As they walked back to the house, Adam kept up a steady stream of conversation. He pointed out both scary and funny Halloween decorations that hung in store windows and talked about Halloweens of his past.

He was rambling, and his rambles only made Melanie's heart ache more. She knew he was trying to keep things normal between them, attempting to fill up any awkward silence that might begin.

But nothing he said, nothing he did could take away the pain that shot through her heart, a pain a hundred times more devastating than the nerve pain in her leg.

He loved her. The words rang in her heart, in her very soul. Whether he truly did or not, when he'd spoken those words to her with his blue eyes shining with emotion, in that moment she'd felt his love washing over her, through her.

He loved her, and she loved him enough to lie and insist that she didn't love him back. She loved him enough to save him from saddling himself with a woman who would always have special needs, who would always need more care than a fully functioning woman. She couldn't do that to him. She refused to do that to him.

For as long as she lived, she would never forget the look on his face when she told him she didn't love him. She would never forget the shock, the disbelief and then the utter pain that had raced across his features. By the time they reached the house, an emotional weariness nearly overwhelmed her.

"Are you okay?" he asked as they stepped through the foyer and he took care of the alarm system.

She had just broken his heart and he was worried about her. She swallowed against a wealth of pain. "I'm fine. Why?"

"You've just become very quiet." His gaze studied her. "I didn't mean to upset you."

"I know." She looked down at her hands in her lap, unable to look at his face. "I just don't want things to change here. I like having you here. You're a great tenant and I'm comfortable with you and I don't want things to become awkward between us."

"They won't," he assured her. "I can't take back what I said to you, and I can't change the way I feel about you, but I can make sure that it doesn't get awkward or crazy between us. I'm a big boy, Melanie. Rejection is a part of life. I'll deal with it. It isn't your problem."

She looked up at him again, a misery she'd never felt before striking deep in her soul. "I'm sorry, Adam." Those words couldn't begin to describe the depth of her sorrow.

He shrugged and offered her a smile. "You can't force matters of the heart." He glanced at his wristwatch. "And now I'm supposed to meet Ben at the shooting range in about a half an hour. Will you be okay here?"

"The sun is shining, and the security is on, so I'll be fine," she assured him. She was actually grateful that he was leaving the house. She needed some time alone to process the myriad emotions that roared through her.

"Then I'll see you later," he said, and just that quickly he was back out the door, leaving only the lingering scent of his cologne behind.

The tears that had begged to be released in the café began to burn in her eyes. Was it possible that he really was in love with her? That somehow he'd been able to see beyond her wheelchair to the woman she was in spite of it?

How badly she wanted to not just accept that he loved her, but also profess her own love for him. How much she wanted to believe that somehow, someway they could build a life and be together forever.

But she didn't.

She thought that if she gave in to her love, allowed Adam into her life on a permanent basis, she would only be destroying the life he was meant to live. He would eventually grow weary of having to lift her in and out of his vehicle. She could give him children, but she couldn't parent them properly from a wheelchair. He needed, he deserved, a soul mate who could walk beside him through life, not one who had to be carried or pushed.

No, it was best that she keep up the charade that she didn't love him. She'd rather dream of what might have been if she were a whole woman than live a dream turned nightmare where Adam would not only fall out of love with her but would secretly come to resent her.

She'd rather live a lonely life than have that happen. It was with a deep, aching loneliness that she went into the kitchen and stared out the back window, her thoughts still racing.

If Adam would just stay as a tenant another two or three months, then she could make a lot of headway on the back taxes owed on the property and she would no longer have to worry so much about losing the house.

But she feared, despite what he'd told her, that things would never go back to normal between them, that all too quickly he'd be ready to move on.

Her cell phone rang, pulling her from her depressing thoughts, and she dug it out of her purse and answered when she saw Tilly's number on the display.

"Hi, Tilly."

"Hey, darling girl. I had planned on coming over today and doing a little cleaning but my knee has been giving me a fit, and so I think it best if I just sit on my butt and keep my leg elevated."

Tilly had arthritis in her knee, and often if there was a weather front moving in, it gave her a lot of pain.

"That's okay," Melanie replied. Secretly she was grateful. She didn't feel like company, not even Tilly could ease the heartache inside her, and she didn't want to pretend and have to put on a happy face. "Besides, I think I'm going to wheel myself down to the grocery store and pick up some candy for the trick-or-treaters."

There was a moment of silence. "Where's Adam?"

"He's out for a while. I'll be fine, Tilly. I can handle an outing that's only a couple of blocks down the sidewalk."

"Are you sure you don't want me to just pick up some candy for you the next time I'm out?"

"Positive," Melanie replied firmly. "Your knee is acting up. You need to rest it. Besides, it will be good for me to take care of this myself." She had to prove to herself that she could be alone, could take care of her own business without any help from anyone. "I'm going to head out in just a few minutes," she continued. "It's a nice day and I'll enjoy the wheelchair stroll."

"Why don't you call me when you get back in? You know I'll worry about you if you don't!" Tilly exclaimed.

Melanie smiled. "Okay, I'll call you when I get back here, but you know there's nothing to worry about. In the meantime turn on the Food Network and keep your leg up and relax."

The two women said goodbye and with a sense of purpose Melanie stuffed her cell phone back into her purse and headed for the front door.

She needed to get out of here, let some fresh air chase the scent of him out of her head. She needed to escape her own thoughts and feelings for just a little while and this first trek on her own to the store was a perfect opportunity to do both.

Her heart thundered an unsteady beat as she opened the front door and she wasn't sure if it was because Adam loved her or because she was about to take her first step all alone out in the real world.

Making sure the alarm system was set, she left the house and wheeled down the ramp to the sidewalk. The thunder of her heart slowed as she gazed toward the grocery store, but the bracing air didn't blow away a single thought of Adam.

As she began to wheel herself down the sidewalk, he filled her head. Each and every smile, the very sound of his laughter swelled in her heart.

If she'd been able to pick and choose the qualities to build a man of her dreams, she knew that in the end it would be Adam. A bump in the sidewalk jarred her and again hot and burdensome tears pressed at her eyes.

She felt like a diabetic plunked down in a candy store with no way to get out. It felt as if fate had especially delivered Adam to her doorstep just to torment her in a game of what might have been.

As she pumped her arms to turn the wheels of her chair, she was vaguely aware of a car passing by her, although she saw nobody else out walking the sidewalks.

Halloween was two days away and goofy ghosts and fanged vampires stared at her from each store window she passed. There was a small seed inside her that knew it would be easier to keep her porch light off and her door firmly closed on Halloween night.

It would break her heart to see each little ghost, every little goblin. Every costumed child would remind her of what she might have had…with Adam.

But she wouldn't keep her door locked and make her house uninviting. She couldn't run from life and she was determined to enjoy the sight of each boy and girl who knocked on her door for candy.

She stopped a moment to rest, realizing that wheeling herself around in her house and a couple of blocks down a sidewalk were two very different things, the latter requiring a lot more upper arm work on her part.

As she came toward the alley that ran between the post office and a little dress boutique, she heard the sound of somebody approaching from behind her.

She wheeled herself toward the alleyway to allow whoever was walking by enough room to pass her on the sidewalk. She forced a smile to her lips and was about to turn in her chair and greet whoever it was when she felt a sharp sting in the side of her neck.

Wasn't it too late in the year for bees or wasps? she thought as she raised her hand to her neck. Her brain instantly became fuzzy. And then there was nothing but darkness reaching out to claim her.

Chapter 15

The shooting range was an indoor arena just outside the city limits of Grady Gulch. It was owned and operated by Linden Walsh, who had served as sheriff of Grady Gulch for almost twenty years before his retirement six years ago.

In the front of the huge building was a retail gun shop run by Linden's wife, Edna, and in the back was as professional a setup for firearm practice as in any big city.

Adam stood in the booth next to Deputy Ben Temple and fired seven times with his 9mm into the paper human target fifteen yards away.

He'd hoped that by coming here, he would work off some of the tumultuous emotions that he'd carried with him when he left Melanie's place.

She didn't love him. How had he misread everything so badly? He'd fallen into the softness he thought he saw in her eyes when she gazed at him. He'd believed the passion in her touch.

He pulled off his headphones and hit the button to move the target toward him so he could check his shots. He had to stop thinking about Melanie and his own foolishness in actually believing she'd be happy to discover that he was in love with her.

The target stopped and Adam gazed at it, noting with satisfaction that all his bullet holes were in a tight circle over the heart of the dark silhouette.

"Nice shooting," Ben said as he stepped up next to Adam. "I'll be sure and tell Cameron that if he decides to take you on as a deputy, at least you know how to hit where you aim."

"Thanks. I appreciate it," Adam replied.

"I'm done for the day. What about you?"

Adam nodded. He'd decided that no matter how many bullets left his gun, they couldn't take away the vast emptiness that had been in his heart since Melanie told him she didn't love him.

"There's a little coffee area in the back. How about we grab a cup?" Ben suggested.

"Sure." It took only minutes for the two to clean up their equipment and then Adam followed Ben to a back room he'd never been in before.

"I didn't even know this was here," he said as he looked around the small area. There were two round tables, several vending machines and a coffeemaker. The aroma indicated that the brew in the carafe was fresh.

"Linden keeps it kind of quiet. He doesn't want a lot of the riffraff that sometimes shows up to know this room is here."

Adam smiled. "So I guess this means I officially pass the riffraff test."

Ben laughed and nodded, then moved over to the coffee and the stack of foam cups. He poured himself a cup and then one for Adam and gestured to a table. Together the two men sat.

"Cameron told me you approached him about becoming a deputy," Ben said.

"I did," Adam confirmed. "It's always been in the back of my mind that it was the job I wanted, but there was the family ranch and then Sam went away, and it hasn't been until the last few weeks that I feel like I'm starting to walk on the path I want for myself."

"The whole thing with Sam…it must have been rough on you and Nick."

"It was," Adam replied. "It still is. His trial is coming up soon."

"Are you hoping for a good outcome?" Ben asked.

Adam took a sip of his coffee and leaned back in his chair. "What he did was wrong and he needs to pay for that. The best outcome for everyone would be for Sam to get time in prison but also to get some mental help. Even after all this time he's still not right." He shrugged. "But it's all going to be up to the court."

"Nick seems to be perfectly happy working your family ranch, especially with Courtney and their little one beside him."

Adam grinned, grateful for the change in topic.

"He's definitely whipped, and he's a very lucky man." The smile fell and he took another sip of the coffee. "How come you haven't married, Ben?"

"Haven't found the right woman yet. Cameron, Jim and I always joke that instead of being the Three Musketeers, we must be more like the Three Stooges, because none of us have managed to find the woman we want to marry." He sipped the hot brew and raised an eyebrow. "What about you?"

"I found the right woman, but apparently I'm the wrong man." Adam forced a lightness to his tone as he fought the utter heaviness in his heart.

"That's tough, man." Ben leaned back in his chair and released a sigh. "Although it's probably good I don't have a girlfriend or a wife right now. We've been working killer hours lately. This is the first real time off I've had since Candy Bailey was murdered. We thought we had our man with Kevin Naperson. The kid seemed good for the crime, but then Shirley Cook wound up dead in the same way."

He shook his head and released a puff of a sigh. "It's been tough on all of us. And now with the attack on Melanie we're all spinning our wheels. Cameron told me to take off for two days and then be prepared to hit it hard again."

"From what he's told me, there's nothing much to investigate."

Ben frowned. "We're all frustrated as hell."

For the next thirty minutes the two sat and talked about the murders of the two waitresses and the attack on Melanie.

"I say that Melanie's attack was done by our man," Ben said. "Everything about the attack was like the others…middle of the night and in through the window. What I don't understand is why he didn't just kill Melanie before she woke up. Why he moved her wheelchair and toyed with her before going after her. That definitely rings of a sadistic nature."

"Was there any evidence at the other two scenes that the killer teased or taunted the women before he killed them?" Adam asked.

"Without an eyewitness to those crimes, it's impossible to know what happened in those rooms before those women were killed but the evidence points to them both being killed in their sleep. We assumed Candy had let her killer into her room, but when we found her dead, she looked as if she'd been killed in her sleep. Maybe he decided to toy with Melanie because he assumed with her wheelchair gone from the side of the bed, she'd be a helpless victim who wouldn't fight back. Maybe he didn't anticipate that she'd wake up before he could kill her."

Ben shrugged. "Or it's possible he's losing control, and murdering sleeping women isn't doing it for him anymore. He has to escalate things now by waking them to get his thrill."

"Some kind of creep," Adam said with a shake of his head. "And the worst part is that he obviously lives here in Grady Gulch. He's one of our own."

"Yeah, sickening, isn't it?"

Twenty minutes later Adam got back in his truck. He didn't immediately start the engine, but rather sat there, unsure whether to go back to the house or find somewhere else to go for the remainder of the day.

She didn't love him.

But he'd thought he'd felt her love so many times, in so many ways, in the past couple of weeks. Had he mistaken her gratitude for love? Apparently so, but it had sure felt like love to him.

He thought about driving to Nick and Courtney's, but he felt too vulnerable to see them right now. The conversation with Ben had been good, and for those minutes when they'd talked about the crimes, he hadn't thought about his heartache.

Being around Nick and Courtney and little Garrett would only remind him of what he couldn't have with the woman he loved. It would only make his heartache resonate deeper, more painfully inside him.

One thing was certain. He wasn't going anywhere. He'd told Melanie that he wouldn't move out, that somehow everything would be fine between them, and no matter how painful that would be for him, he'd make sure it happened for her.

He had to figure out a way to look at her as his landlady, not as the woman he loved. He'd signed up for a couple of classes over the internet and he'd focus on that. Then in January his classes would begin at the community college and that would keep him busy and out of the house. Surely that would make things easier.

He also planned to follow up on his offer to financially back her new venture of costume making. He knew she'd be a big success and he had no qualms about becoming a business partner with her. What he didn't want to think about too deeply was if he still intended to do it owing to the fact that it would keep her somehow bound to him.

All he had to do was get through the next couple of days, the next few months, and then he'd be able to focus full-time on pursuing the work he wanted to do for the rest of his life. In the meantime he'd do what he could to help out at the family ranch, which still provided much of his financial stability.

He decided to head back to the house. Staying away would only make things more awkward when he finally returned there. Under normal circumstances he'd be ready to head back there for some lunch.

He started the truck and headed back to town and Melanie's house. Maybe he'd professed his love for her too soon. Maybe if he'd waited another week, another month, her reply might have been different.

A tiny ray of hope lit his heart at this thought. Just because she didn't love him now didn't mean he couldn't try everything possible to make her fall in love with him.

Time. Maybe it wasn't a matter of right woman, wrong man. Maybe he'd simply rushed things, not given their relationship enough time to grow and flourish.

That tiny ray of hope burned a little brighter. Maybe there was still a chance to wind up with the woman he wanted to spend the rest of his life with. Maybe it would just take more effort and patience.

As he pulled into the driveway, he cautioned himself and tried to tamp down some of the hope, knowing he might possibly be setting himself up for a new heartbreak.

Adam didn't know a lot about love, but he was smart enough to know that there was an element about it that was inexplicable, that sometimes there was no way to explain why people loved each other and why they didn't.

Chemistry. He'd felt it the very first time he'd laid eyes on Melanie. But had she felt any of that same heart-pumping attraction?

He turned off the truck and got out, for a moment standing next to it as his left hand snaked into his jacket pocket and toyed with the plastic chips.

He stuffed back the pain that radiated from his heart and pasted a pleasant smile on his face as he approached the front door.

Opening the door using his key set off the tinny *beep, beep* of the alarm and he quickly moved to the control panel and punched in the numbers to prevent the alarm from going off.

"Melanie?" he called as he went into the living room. "Just wanted to let you know that I'm back."

There was no answering reply. He went into the kitchen but she wasn't there, either. Her bedroom door was closed, and he stared at it for a long moment, wondering if perhaps she was napping.

Still, hadn't she heard him come in? He didn't like the fact that she hadn't responded in any way to his call. Maybe he was being overly paranoid, because this was the first time she'd been left alone since the attack.

He stood just outside her bedroom door and called

her name once again. "Melanie?" He knocked softly, and when there was still no reply, he opened the door, surprised to find the room empty.

The bathroom door was open, indicating that she wasn't in there, either. So where was she? He tamped down an edge of panic that had begun to thrum inside him.

There were no signs anywhere in the rooms that would indicate she was in trouble. He walked to the front door and stared outside. He'd built a ramp for her so she could leave the house whenever she wanted. Obviously she'd finally decided to use it on her own.

He wondered what time she'd left and where she was going. He hoped she hadn't attempted to go too far on this first trip alone. The times they'd gone to the café, he'd had to push her home partway because her arms had tired.

Maybe he should just take a little walk. She'd mentioned having to get some candy for Halloween, so it was possible she'd decided to go to the grocery store.

He could head that way, and if he saw her and she was doing fine, then he could pretend he was going to the store for something. If she looked weary, then he could help her get back home.

Decision made, he left the house once again and headed down the sidewalk in the direction of the Shop and Go grocery store. As he gazed down toward the store, he didn't see her on the sidewalk, but that didn't concern him. It was possible she was already in the store and it was possible she hadn't gone to get candy but had decided to have a cup of coffee at the café or whatever.

He told himself the little edge of worry that was trying to work through him was due simply to the fact that he hadn't forgotten the sound of her screams, the horrifying sight of her as he pulled her out of her closet on the night of the attack. But it was the middle of the day and there was no reason to be concerned.

There was no reason to be concerned until he reached the alley and glanced down it. He froze, the thunder of his heart making the sound of anything else inaudible.

Her wheelchair. He knew it was hers by the tiny pink dancer that hung from one of the handles.

It was halfway into the alley, half hidden by a Dumpster. Why would she have gone into the alley? What was she doing there?

Melanie. Her name resounded in his head as he broke his inertia and raced toward the chair, the chair that he already knew was empty.

Maybe she'd somehow fallen out of it. Maybe she'd been lying in the dirty alley, crying for help, waiting for somebody to find her.

"Melanie!" he shouted as he ran, but it took only one look at the chair and its immediate surroundings for him to recognize that she wasn't there. What was there was her purse. It lay on the ground next to the chair.

He didn't touch it. He didn't touch anything as he backed up, fumbling in his coat pocket for his cell phone. It was a crime scene, his brain screamed. Melanie was in trouble.

As he punched in the number that would alert the authorities, he tried to make sense of it all. Maybe she had grown tired and had called somebody to come and get her. He immediately dismissed the idea. Melanie wouldn't have gone with somebody and left her purse behind.

When his call was answered, he quickly gave his location and said that he needed the sheriff and every deputy in the area to respond.

With the call made, he stood at the mouth of the alley, fear nearly casting him to his knees. Where could she be? Who had taken her? And most importantly of all, were they already too late to save her?

Melanie came to with the smell of pasture under her nose and a pounding in her head that made her nauseous. For several long minutes she remained unmoving, waiting for the headache to abate, for the fogginess in her brain to dissipate enough so that she could think.

What was happening? Where was she and how had she gotten here? She fought to work through the cotton that felt wrapped around her brain, cutting her off from reality.

She opened one eye in a narrow slit, unsurprised to find earth beneath her. She sensed somebody nearby but was afraid to turn over on her back, afraid to see who was with her before she figured out what had happened.

Closing her eye again, she tried to think.

Halloween. She'd been on her way to the store to pick up candy. Adam had told her he loved her. Her thoughts froze on that single thought. Adam had told her he loved her and she'd rejected him and now she was on the ground someplace and didn't know how she got here or what was happening to her.

She'd been on her way to the store. She had sensed somebody walking behind her and had moved over to allow them to pass. A sting in the neck and then nothing.

She fought against a deep sob that threatened to burst forth from her. Obviously she'd been drugged by that little bee sting in the neck. How long had she been unconscious?

Cold. She was so cold. She no longer wore the coat she'd had on when she left the house. An uncontrollable shudder propelled through her as she recognized she was in trouble. She thought she might be in big trouble.

"I know you're conscious," a deep voice said from nearby.

It was a familiar voice, and with a sharp intake of breath she opened her eyes and rolled over on her back. She sat up and looked at the man who had orchestrated this new terror.

Deputy Jim Collins looked neat and professional in his khaki uniform. The midday sun glinted off his deputy badge. She shot a glance around, still trying to absorb everything.

She was in the center of a vast overgrown pasture. There were no outbuildings in sight. In the far distance she saw an old tractor that looked as if it hadn't been ridden in years, his patrol car and the decaying carcass of a dead cow. She looked back at him in horror.

"That's old Nelly," he said as he pointed to the dead

cow. "She had a bad limp in her left front leg, couldn't walk very well, and so I brought her here and shot her."

The reference to a bad leg certainly wasn't lost on her and a new terror threatened to take hold of her. Did he intend to shoot her like he had his cow and leave her body out here to decompose?

"Jim, what's going on? Why am I here?" And where was here? she wondered as she stared at Jim.

His brown eyes seemed to darken to black coals. "You're here because this is where you belong." He shoved his hands in his pants pockets, a tension seeming to swell his body beneath the official jacket that he wore. "My parents gave me this land when I was sixteen. It was for me to build my dream family home."

She frowned, trying to focus on his words and not on the panic that made it hard for her to breathe, the panic that made it impossible not to focus on how rough the dirt was beneath her palms as she braced herself up. "I don't understand. What does this have to do with me?"

"Everything!" The word exploded from him as if it was a bullet shot from a gun. "I was going to build my dream house here and you were supposed to be here with me. We were going to get married and have children and be a happy family together."

"What are you talking about?" Melanie felt as if the world had suddenly become an alien place, that he was part of the landscape, a dangerous subspecies of human spouting a language she didn't understand.

"We dated. We were in love and we were going have a perfect life together." He jerked his hands from his pockets and took a step closer to her, his eyes blazing with anger, with a bitter betrayal.

She stared up at him in astonishment. What on earth was he talking about? "Jim, we went out a couple of times, but it was nothing more than a few casual dates. I never told you I loved you, that I wanted to marry you."

"Yes, you did! You did tell me that you loved me." Spittle flew from his mouth as he screamed the words.

"When? When did I tell you that?" she cried, her heart beating so fast, it felt as if it might pop right out of her chest.

"On graduation day. I hugged you and told you I loved you, and you told me you loved me, too. You loved me and then you left. You didn't just leave me, but you left the whole town for some stupid dream that you thought was so much more important than me and our love."

Speechless, she stared at him as her mind went back in time to the day of graduation. After the final cap toss in the air, bedlam had reigned and all the students had been hugging family members and fellow students. There had been plenty of "I love yous" thrown around, along with promises to be best friends, lovers and/or partners forever.

Had she told Jim "I love you, too"? Possibly. She'd probably also said those very same words to dozens of girls and boys that day. She'd been euphoric on graduation day, aware that it was finally her time to pursue the dream of dancing she'd held close to her heart since she was a child.

Before she could say anything, he continued, pacing

about ten feet from where she was propped up on the hard earth. "All through our junior and senior year I worked to draw up the plans for our house. I fantasized about our wedding day. Whenever we were together, I saw the way you looked at me and I knew that all my dreams would come true."

He was screaming now, his pleasant features twisted into a Halloween mask of monster rage. "And then you just left. Without a word, without any regard for me and my plans. You just left, like the selfish bitch you are."

She was stunned by the vitriol that poured from him. Sick. He was sick in the head, she realized, and as she smelled the scent of death that came from the cow, she feared Jim's next move.

"Jim, I'm sorry if I hurt you. That was never my intention." Her voice trembled uncontrollably. "Was it you who broke into my bedroom?"

For a moment his rage faded and a small smile played on his lips. "Scared you, didn't I? I got a big hoot out of coming in and out of your bedroom window a couple of times. I moved your teakettle, just to mess with your mind." His eyes became hard, flat pebbles once again. "And I smashed those pictures of you on the wall."

Another smile played on his lips. "But I particularly enjoyed breaking in and moving your wheelchair, trying to get you out of that closet and then being called to investigate the crime."

The smile vanished and once again his eyes grew dark and cold. "I would have eventually got to you that night if Adam hadn't come home when he had. I was going to put you back in your bed and slice your throat. Your death would have been written up as yet another one attributed to the killer we're already looking for."

Hopelessness washed over her. Nobody would ever suspect Jim of breaking the law in any way. He was a respected deputy. She glanced over to the dead cow once again and then back at Jim.

"Don't worry. I'm not going to shoot you. I'm not even going to cut your throat," he assured her.

"You can just drive me back to town and we can forget about all of this," she said desperately. "I won't tell anyone. I promise, Jim. This can all be our little secret."

"Yeah, right," he said dryly. "Fate has already given you a taste of the punishment you deserve. You left me to dance and now you can't anymore, but it's not enough. You deserve so much more punishment for destroying my dreams."

"What are you going to do to me?" she asked fearfully. Any fog in her brain that might have existed after she initially regained consciousness was long gone, replaced by the icy chill of panic.

"I'm not going to kill you," he replied. "This is the land where we were supposed to live together, the place where we'd eventually be buried together. We're fifteen miles out of town and the nearest neighbor is seven miles down the road. You can scream your fool head off and nobody is going to hear you."

He looked around the property and then returned his gaze to her. "There's no water on the property, no food, and the forecast is for it to dip below freezing tonight. You can't walk. You're nothing but a useless cripple. I don't have to kill you myself. All I have to do is drive away and leave you here. I figure it will only take three or four days for you to die of dehydration or hypothermia, and that's only if the coyotes don't get you. They're thick out here and hungry."

"Jim, please…" Tears filled her eyes as she realized his intention. "Please, don't leave me out here."

"You left me all alone for the last ten years." His voice rose slightly, the rage again shining in his eyes. "You broke my heart. You ruined me for any other woman."

Without warning he leapt forward and slammed his boot down on her good ankle. Melanie screamed in pain and attempted to roll away from him, but his boot came down again and again, until there was nothing but pain and her screams and finally blessed unconsciousness.

Chapter 16

Adam was beside himself as he watched Cameron, Ben Temple and two other deputies process the scene around the wheelchair. Cameron had called in every deputy he had on the payroll, and although Adam knew it wouldn't be long before the streets were crawling with lawmen asking questions, it wouldn't be quickly enough.

His head and his heart screamed that Melanie was in deep trouble, and with each minute that ticked by, the odds of finding her alive and well seemed to diminish. Something had to be done. Something had to be done right now, but there was no way to hurry the process.

With each deputy that arrived on scene, Cameron barked out orders, the strain on everyone's face showing their frustration at the lack of clues.

With everyone working, Cameron broke away from the group and grabbed Adam's arm. "Let's head back to her house. We'll make that the place for everyone to check in as they have something to report." Cameron raised his collar against a cold wind that had begun to blow in the last hour or so.

Adam frowned. "I don't want to be cooped up in the house. I need to be out searching for her. She needs me," he said desperately. He had to do something, whatever it took to find her and bring her home safe.

"And where are you going to start searching for her?" Cameron asked kindly.

Adam gazed at him hollowly as reality slammed into him. "I wouldn't even know where to begin to search."

Cameron clapped him on the back. "The best place for both of us to be at the moment is at Melanie's house to coordinate our search and gather information. Besides, maybe somebody will call, somebody who knows where she is or saw what happened to her. Maybe somebody wants ransom money for her safe return. You need to be there to answer the phone."

Adam nodded numbly and together he and Cameron started down the sidewalk. Neither of them spoke and Adam suspected Cameron's mind was as jumbled as his, that Cameron was as confused as he was about what might have taken place in that alley.

Melanie. His heart cried out her name. How had Melanie gotten there in the first place? She wouldn't have willingly pushed herself in an alley that smelled of trash. Somebody had forced her in there. But who? And why?

Adam opened the door to the house and immediately entered the security code to unarm the system. He had a feeling there were going to be a lot of people in and out and there was no point in keeping it on at the moment. The worst had already happened.

And it hadn't happened in the middle of the night. It hadn't happened in her bedroom. Danger had found her in the middle of the day on Main Street in Grady Gulch.

Emptiness shouted in the house, the absence of Melanie screaming from every corner. Adam paced the kitchen floor as Cameron checked the answering machine for any messages. There was one from Tilly.

"Melanie, are you home yet? It's been almost an hour and a half since you left. Surely you should have made it to the grocery store and back by now. Are you there?" There was an audible sigh of worry. "Well, call me the minute you get in."

"Call her back," Cameron said. "Find out exactly what Melanie said to her before she left here."

Adam nodded. He punched in Tilly's number, and when the older woman answered, Cameron hit the speakerphone button so that both of them could hear.

"Tilly, it's Adam."

"Adam! Is Melanie with you?"

"No. What time did you talk to her, Tilly?" Adam held the phone tightly against his ear.

"It was a couple of hours ago." Tilly's worry was evident in her voice. "Are you at the house? She was just going to the store to pick up some candy for Halloween. She should have been home by now."

"Tilly, something has happened. We found Melanie's

wheelchair in the alley halfway to the grocery store. We don't know where she is or what's happened to her."

"Oh, Lordy, I'm on my way."

Before Adam could say another word, Tilly hung up. Adam replaced the receiver with a look at Cameron. "So we know she left here about two hours ago to go to the store for candy. And that's all we know." He walked into the living room and sank down on the sofa, his legs unable to hold him upward as a cold wind of despair blew through him.

"Adam, it's only one-thirty in the afternoon. We have plenty of daylight left to tear this town apart," Cameron said firmly. "We'll find her."

"Whoever took her has a two-hour head start on us. She could be out of the damned county by now!" Adam exclaimed in frantic frustration.

Cameron didn't answer, as at that moment his cell phone rang. As he spoke to whoever the caller was, Adam got up off the sofa and paced the living room floor.

The photographs of Melanie on the wall haunted him. She was memorialized in them, so vital, so alive. He remembered dancing with her, the beauty of her movements, the shine that had lit her eyes. Her lack of mobility in one leg had dimmed her light for months, but in the past couple of weeks Adam had seen her love of life returning, a new hope filling her eyes.

The idea that somebody now intended to take that away from her was like a piercing arrow through his heart. He wanted the time with her, time to show her that he was the right man for her, that nobody would ever love her as he did.

If he couldn't convince her that they belonged together, he wanted her to find love with somebody else, to build a future and a family that would enrich her soul as she lived her life.

He stopped in his tracks as the front door flew open and Tilly came in.

"Have you found her?"

Adam shook his head, too devastated to reply verbally. Tilly began to weep and Adam reached out and pulled the bony older woman into his arms, feeling as if she were crying the tears from his aching heart.

"We'll find her, Tilly," he said, finally releasing her as her sobs began to subside.

"Who would do something like this? Who would be so evil?" She sank down on the sofa and looked from Adam to Cameron. "You have to find her, Cameron. She can't walk. She can't run. There's no way she can escape from somebody who is holding her."

"We're doing everything we can," Cameron replied as he dropped his cell phone in his pocket. "That was Jim. He's talking to all the shopkeepers along Main Street to see if anyone saw anything. We know now she never made it to the grocery store, so whoever took her did so as she was heading to the store."

They all turned toward the window at the sound of the wind whistling around the side of the house. It sounded cold and bleak, and Adam felt the icy chill seeping through his very bones as he thought of Melanie.

The next couple of hours were sheer agony. Tilly

busied herself keeping the coffee hot and making sandwiches for the deputies who came in to report to Cameron, while Adam stood at the window, his brain racing for answers that refused to appear.

He hadn't seen any danger when he left the house. He hadn't sensed that his absence would put her at risk in any way. Otherwise he would have never left her alone. He'd thought she'd be safe.

"This is so unlike the man you've been chasing," he said to Cameron when the latest report of nothing had come in. "Why has he changed how he operates? Why would he attempt to go after Melanie again if it meant doing everything different than he's done before? Why take such a risk to kidnap her off Main Street instead of waiting until nightfall and taking somebody else?" Adam frowned at his own questions as he waited for Cameron to respond.

The sheriff raked his hand through his hair and drew a deep breath. "I don't know. This all doesn't make sense if we look at his previous pattern."

"And you're sure Kevin Naperson wasn't responsible for the first two murders?" Adam asked, knowing the young man had been suspected in the first murder.

"At first he was the best suspect we had when Candy was murdered and we thought it might be possible that he killed Shirley to take the heat off himself for Candy's death, but since then my gut instinct has made me doubt he was involved in either murder."

"Maybe this isn't your killer at all," Adam said thoughtfully. "Maybe this really is something personal. We need to find Craig Jenkins," he said urgently. "He's the only person who really has anything to gain by Melanie being dead."

"Already on it," Cameron replied. "Mike Waddell is on his way to Evanston to find Jenkins." He looked at his wristwatch. "If Jenkins has Melanie, then we should know something in the next twenty minutes or so."

At that moment Jim Collins walked in the door and Adam could tell by the grim expression on his face that he had no news.

"Nobody I talked to in the stores or on the streets saw anything. They didn't see Melanie. They didn't see anybody acting strange or out of the ordinary. It's like some giant bird swooped out of the sky and picked her up."

"Yeah, well, if I find out the name of that bird, I'm going to kill him," Adam replied, his voice not raging with vengeance but rather calm with unmistakable promise.

Pain. Excruciating pain brought Melanie slowly back to consciousness. She raised herself up and with trembling fingers pulled down her sock to look at the damage. She gasped as she saw the swollen, bruised skin. Her ankle felt broken…shattered. She began to weep with the sharp pain and the fear that now she had two feet that couldn't work.

She had no idea how long she was lost in a sea of sobs. She lay on the ground in a fetal ball and cried until she could cry no more.

Finally she rolled onto her back and winced at the hardness of the ground beneath her as she stared up at the sky. A cold breeze had begun to blow, sending bright blue clouds dancing across the sky. Blue…like Adam's eyes.

Her heart constricted painfully. She'd never see him again. She'd never see anyone again. She would become a mystery in town. Whatever happened to Melanie Brooks? People would talk about her disappearance in the café, wonder while shopping in the stores where the killer had taken her, where he had possibly buried her.

Adam would be devastated. She squeezed her eyes closed tightly once again. She knew with a woman's intuition that her disappearance would haunt him for a long time to come. But eventually he'd move on. He'd find the right woman, a woman who could walk beside him, run after his children and be the partner he deserved.

She'd hoped that thought would bring her happiness, but it didn't. She didn't want to think about Adam with another woman. She would die out here knowing that he was the man for her, her soul mate, and she'd been foolish enough to reject him, reject what might have been.

Craig Jenkins would win. Her death would assure that he got her house. Anger drove her up to a sitting position once again and she slammed her hand against her bad leg.

A useless cripple. That was what Jim had called her and that was what she was, nothing but a helpless cripple. It was because of this that it had been so easy for Jim to take her, so easy for him to bring her here and assure her death.

Thank God he hadn't touched her other than stomping on her foot. He was crazy. As crazy as some of the mental cases she'd seen wandering or panhandling in Times Square when she lived in the big city. If he had tried to kiss her, had attempted to molest her in any way, she would have died on the spot.

Nobody would know that she wasn't a new victim of the killer who had been on everyone's mind. Nobody would realize that one of the men sworn to protect the town suffered from a deep obsession with her and there was no reason why in the future he wouldn't do the same thing with another woman.

She hated that Cameron wouldn't know that there was not one killer, but two in the town he loved. She hated that he would never know that one of his trusted deputies was twisted enough to kill.

She wrapped her arms around herself as the wind seemed to pierce through her. An icy shiver walked up her spine and she bit back more threatening tears as the stabbing pain in her ankle continued.

Tears would accomplish nothing. She could accomplish nothing. All she could do was sit here and wait for death to claim her. Already she was thirsty, as if knowing that she couldn't have a drink had mentally created a massive thirst.

She'd go mad before death ever came, she thought as she gazed around the empty pasture. How long would it take her to die out here all alone? Days? A week? A frantic sob once again escaped her.

Helpless cripple.

She didn't want to be that person. She was so much

more than that. She took care of her own needs. She cooked for herself, cleaned the downstairs of her house. She laughed, she cried and she loved. She was a person, not a cripple.

Adam. His name sang through her. She'd thought of herself as a useless prisoner in a wheelchair until he'd come along. He'd opened the world to her again, building her a ramp to leave her prison, showing her a way she could make a living once again and allowing her to dance in his arms.

When he looked at her, she knew he didn't see a helpless cripple. He saw a woman he desired, a strong woman who he believed was capable of doing anything she set her mind to. And she was that woman. She had to believe that.

Once again she looked around, desperate to find some way to help herself, unwilling to simply sit in the middle of the field and wait for death to find her.

Jim couldn't have thought of a better way to torture her than to leave her here. A bullet to the head would have been kinder than the slow, agonizing punishment he'd given her.

In the distance she saw a stand of trees. She might have found them a windbreak against the cold air blowing from the north, but they might as well be a hundred miles away.

She looked in the opposite direction and her gaze landed on the tractor. It looked as distant as the trees and once again she was overwhelmed with her inadequacies.

She had a leg that wouldn't work and now an ankle

through which pain continued to shoot, as if all the bones inside had been crunched.

Once again she looked at the tractor. It looked as if it hadn't been used for a long time, but what if it would run? What if it could be her means of escape?

The very idea seemed ridiculous. Even if it did run, she'd still have to get to it, and that wasn't possible. Nothing was possible because she was a useless cripple.

Stop it. The voice thundered in her head. It was Adam's voice that spoke in her brain. "Stop thinking like that," she murmured aloud, this time with a surge of strength rising up.

Adam had told her she could be and do anything she wanted, that she was strong and stubborn and was capable of anything she set her mind to doing.

She looked at the tractor once again. It might not run. It might be a relic left dead in the field. She couldn't know whether it might help her or not until she got closer.

She had two choices…sit here and wait for death or attempt to move herself to the tractor and hope and pray that the key was in the ignition and that it would work.

Standing up was certainly out of the question, but so was being a passive participant in her own death. She'd managed to move across her bedroom floor like a crab when Jim entered her bedroom in the dead of night. She could work her way across the pasture the same way, moving backward and dragging her legs across the hard earth.

She attempted this, crying out in pain as her wounded ankle bumped against the ground. Gasping, and then trying to regulate her breathing with slow, even breaths, she reminded herself that she'd lived with the pain of peripheral neuropathy for the past seven months. She could rise above the pain in her other ankle because she had to, because she had no other choice.

Despite the cold wind that chilled her body as she began once again to drag herself, beads of sweat popped out along her brow. With each move she made, she moaned and yelped like a wounded animal.

She stopped only when her arms were exhausted from her efforts. A hysterical burst of laughter threatened to escape her as she realized she'd managed to move herself only about six feet. At this rate it would take her until nightfall to make it there.

Once again she fought against a wave of hopelessness. At least if she made it to the tractor, she could hopefully pull herself up in the seat and she wouldn't be easy pickings if any hungry coyotes showed up.

Besides, despite the futility of it all, she refused to give up. She'd survived the trauma that had put her in a wheelchair. She'd be damned if she'd just succumb to Jim's plot to get revenge for a perceived betrayal without fighting for her life.

Once again she began to move, and when she tired of dragging herself backward, she rolled over on her stomach and pulled herself along the ground that way.

Agony. She was in sheer agony as sticks and rocks stabbed her legs, as her shoulders and arms screamed with the effort of moving forward inch by inch.

She tried to rise above the pain, filling her head with thoughts of Adam. He'd been the gift that fate had blown into her life. She had been a sour, cranky cripple before he moved in, but he'd transformed her with his smiles, with the quiet assurances that she was so much more than the box she'd put herself in. He was supposed to have been just the cowboy upstairs, but he had become so much more to her.

If she died, she'd die knowing that he'd been her hero, the man who had made her want to be better than what she was, the man who had made her want to strive for more.

The wind had gotten colder, and as she rested for a moment, it inched into her and she shivered with a chill that penetrated her bones.

Overhead the sun had disappeared beneath a layer of clouds that had begun to invade the sky, but she knew the forecast wasn't for rain, but rather just dismal late afternoon clouds, a blustery late October afternoon and evening.

Inch by excruciating inch she moved forward, her gaze never leaving the tractor in the distance. When she realized she'd moved half the distance from the place she'd been dumped to the tractor, a sudden burst of euphoria filled her, momentarily taking away her pain.

She could do this. She was capable of doing so much more than she'd thought she could, so much more than Jim believed she could.

She consciously willed herself not to consider that the tractor wouldn't run, that she might not be able to operate it as a means of escape. At the moment the farm equipment simply represented a goal she was determined to reach.

As she drew closer to the tractor, she realized it didn't look as old as she'd initially thought, and her hope reached new limits.

Was it possible that the tractor might run? Was it possible Jim had so underestimated her strength and will that he'd left a means of escape in the pasture?

The idea forced her to move faster as she realized dusk would be arriving soon and after that night. She knew out here with no moon or stars the darkness would be profound. She had to reach the tractor before that happened.

She renewed her efforts, pain a constant companion as she inched her way closer and closer to the tractor. *You can do it.* It was Adam's deep voice that rang in her head, that sang through her veins.

You can do it. It was her voice, owning the physical and emotional strength she knew she possessed. She understood pain, had danced with it many times, had nursed it between rehearsals. Pain had no place in a dancer's life and so she'd willed herself not to feel, and that was exactly what she did now. The show must go on.

The purple shadows of dusk were painting the western sky when she finally touched the faded green metal of the foot rung on the tractor. For a moment all she could do was simply cling to it with her hand, too exhausted to do anything else.

Filth covered her and her jeans were torn, bloody knees showing through, but she'd made it. She'd made it! *But you aren't free yet,* a little voice whispered inside her.

From the ground the seat and the steering wheel looked miles high. A glance at the ankle that Jim had stomped assured her that there was no way she would be able to bear weight on it. She'd have to use the strength of her arms and shoulders to hoist herself up.

From her vantage point she couldn't tell if there was a key in the ignition or not, and therefore she had no idea if this had simply been a futile crawl of pain.

There was only one way to find out. Using both her hands, she hoisted herself up and twisted so that she was now seated on the metal rung. Still she couldn't see if there was a key in the ignition. It wasn't uncommon for ranchers to leave keys in their equipment. Code of honor and all that still existed in Grady Gulch...except when it came to men like Jim and the killer, who still remained unknown.

She rested for several long moments, wondering if her arms and shoulders would ever not ache again. She stared down at her feet, one pointed daintily down to the ground and the other with an ankle that was now twice the size it should be.

Now or never, she thought as she eyed the steering wheel. She used to be able to do pull-ups when she was dancing. She and a couple of other dancers had belonged to a gym and had worked out whenever they had a chance.

One pull-up. That's all you need to do, she told herself. She drew several deep breaths, reaching for every ounce of strength she had inside her.

Extension—it was part of dance. Long extensions of arms and legs to make a perfect graceful line. There was no grace in the line Melanie made as she threw herself upward and grabbed on to the steering wheel.

Her arms felt as if they were being pulled out of her shoulder sockets as she hung for a moment, and then with a burst of adrenaline and a cry of a warrior, she pulled herself up and into the seat.

She trembled from head to toe, exhausted by her efforts, but when she saw the old rusty key in the ignition, a new burst of adrenaline surged inside her.

Please, she begged whatever higher power might be watching, might be listening. *Please let this work.* Her hand shook as she reached for the key. It was icy cold between her fingers, and holding her breath, she turned it.

Nothing happened.

As she realized all her efforts, all the pain and sweat, had been for nothing, she laid her head down on the steering wheel and wept.

Chapter 17

As the sun sank lower in the west, Adam's heart sank, as well. Too much time had passed since Melanie had disappeared for him to be able to summon much hope. Soon it would be dark and he couldn't stand the thought of her out someplace in the night.

He stood in the kitchen, at the window, staring out at the deepening shadows, and his heart cried out in pain. Cameron's men had been pounding the sidewalks, talking to shopkeepers and neighbors, but nobody had seen anything.

As word got out of Melanie's disappearance, people began to stop by the house, offering to help. Even Brandon Williams in his motorized scooter zoomed up the ramp and asked what he could do to help with the investigation.

But there was nothing anyone could do. She was gone and they had no idea how to find her. He leaned his forehead against the window, the pane cold against his skin.

Melanie, where are you? Somehow they'd missed something, overlooked a crucial piece of evidence.

In the pit of his gut Adam didn't believe they were chasing the person who had killed two waitresses in the previous months. The more he thought about everything, the more he became convinced that this was something personal.

Somebody had tried to destroy the photos of her that hung on the living room wall, photos of her doing what she'd loved best at that time in her life. Dancing was what had taken her away from Grady Gulch. Had somebody been angry when she left? Angry enough to carry a grudge for ten long years?

He jumped as a hand touched the back of his shirt. He turned to see Tilly, tired lines etched in her face. "Come and grab a sandwich, Adam. You haven't eaten anything all day."

He shook his head. "I'm not hungry, but thanks, anyway."

"She'd want you to eat, Adam," Tilly replied reproachfully.

Adam tightened his hands into fists at his sides. "She'd want me to find her." He turned back to stare outside, wondering how long his heart could beat so frantically, how long he could hold out any kind of hope that they'd find her alive.

They were missing something. He knew that Cameron was covering all the bases. Craig Jenkins had been in the middle of a meeting in Evanston at the time that Melanie had disappeared. Denver Walton had been having a leisurely lunch with Maddy Billings, and Billy Vickers had been delivering mail.

Adam turned around and gazed at the scene before him. Cameron and Jim Collins were seated at the table, going over the list of people who had been interviewed, the places that had been searched.

Melanie had insisted she hadn't dated anyone seriously before she left Grady Gulch. She'd mentioned only three names: Denver Walton, Billy Vickers and Jim Collins.

He narrowed his gaze as he studied the pleasant-looking deputy. Nobody had questioned Jim concerning the disappearance. Where had Jim been at the time Melanie had vanished?

Adam's mind clicked and whirled. Adam knew personally about obsession and revenge. His brother had waited two long years before attacking. Sam had simmered with rage and the need for revenge for a long time before he finally exploded.

Was it possible Jim had some kind of a grudge against Melanie? One that had simmered for years and had been acted on only when she came back to town?

It seemed crazy, and yet it was the only theory that hadn't been explored. The more Adam thought about it, the more he couldn't let it go. Jim had never married. Adam couldn't remember anyone he'd even dated.

He motioned to Cameron. "Could I speak to you for just a minute?"

Immediately Cameron got up from the table and walked over to where Adam stood.

"Let's go into the bedroom," Adam said and gestured to Melanie's room.

The minute Adam stepped into the room, his heart once again squeezed tight in his chest, making it hard for him to take a deep breath. The room held her scent and he wanted nothing more than to crawl into the bed where they had made love, lose himself in the memories of having her in his arms.

Instead he turned to look at Cameron. "Has anyone checked out where Jim was when Melanie disappeared?"

Cameron gave him a look of surprise, but the look quickly changed into a thoughtful frown. "Jim lives in a one-bedroom apartment. If he took Melanie, there's no way he could get her inside there without somebody seeing him. Besides, he's been here since word got out that she was missing. If he's here, then where is Melanie?"

Dead. The terrible word blew through Adam on a wind of despair and he could tell by the expression on Cameron's face that the same word had entered his mind.

"Is there any place he could have taken her? He could be keeping her locked up or something while he's here," Adam continued, driven by need. "He's the only one we haven't checked out, Cameron. I know he's a deputy and all, but he's a final piece that needs investigating. Where specifically was he at the time when Melanie was taken?"

"I don't know. He was on duty but I can't know specifically what part of town he was in or what he was doing at the time." Cameron stared at Adam for a long moment. "He has some property off of County Road J. He's always talked about building a house there, but as far as I know, he's never done anything with it. I'll send some men out there to check it out."

Adam grabbed Cameron's arm. "No! I'll go. I don't want Jim to know that we're checking it out. You can tell him I'm heading back to my family ranch, that I need to be with Nick and Courtney." An urgency gripped him by the throat. "Just let me do this, Cameron. That way if there's nothing there, then Jim won't be the wiser, and while I'm gone, you can use your team to pursue any other leads."

Cameron stared at him for several long moments and then finally gave a curt nod of his head. "The property is on the left side of the road about ten, twelve miles outside of town. Call me the minute you get there."

Adam didn't wait for him to change his mind. He walked out of Melanie's room, across the living room to the front door and then broke into a run toward his truck.

It was probably a wild-goose chase, he thought as he backed out of the driveway and then roared down the street. Cameron still had plenty of men knocking on doors in Grady Gulch, checking abandoned storefronts and sheds, anywhere a woman could be stashed away.

Somebody could find her before Adam even made it to Jim's property, and as long as they found her alive, that would be perfectly fine with Adam.

He just wanted her back. He needed her back. In the hours that she'd been missing, he'd realized that it was his love for Melanie that had suddenly focused his life.

In the past couple of weeks he'd looked at himself as a man and realized his anger about Sam had gone on too long, that it was time for him to look forward instead of backward. The fact that Melanie functioned so well from her wheelchair shamed him into wanting more for himself.

How could he ever get a chance to win her love if somebody killed her? How could he hope to win the heart of a dead woman?

His heart thrummed a frantic rhythm as he barreled down Main Street and headed toward the turnoff that would place him on County Road J. He knew the road… rarely traveled except for the people who lived there, a lot of fields on either side, with the houses few and far between.

It seemed almost impossible to believe that Jim could be involved in this…*almost* impossible. But there was a small possibility that he could be involved.

Adam stepped on the gas, afraid that he was too late, afraid not to hurry in spite of his fears. He turned on his headlights against the darkening gloom of night.

He couldn't stand the idea of Melanie not being home, not being where she belonged throughout the endless night. He patted his cell phone, assuring himself that it was in his pocket and knowing that Cameron would call him immediately if anything happened in town.

He'd made so many mistakes…. They'd made so

many mistakes. Everyone had just assumed they were chasing the same killer who had struck before. But Adam should have known something about the attack was different. He should have realized when he saw the broken glass on the pictures on the wall and when Melanie couldn't remember doing it that something evil was present.

Clenching his hands tightly on the steering wheel, he cursed himself for not realizing she wasn't safe anywhere, that the person who wanted her could strike at any time, in any place.

He should have never told her he loved her. He should have never left the house to go to the shooting range. He'd let her down.

And the night was getting darker. Out here there were no streetlamps and the only lights he saw came from the houses he occasionally passed.

As he turned off onto the county road, he glanced down at his odometer, checking the numbers for reference. Cameron had said Jim's land was ten to twelve miles down the road on the left.

He had to slow his speed. The road was narrow, with potholes and crumbling asphalt on either side. He wanted to fly for the next ten miles, but instead he eased off the gas pedal and wondered how he'd even see her in the encroaching darkness.

He'd have to walk with a flashlight and yell her name, he thought. He'd have to hope and pray that she was in good enough condition to respond to his cries.

If only Cameron would call and tell him they'd found

her and she was okay. But by the time he hit the ten-mile marker, there had been no phone call.

He stopped the truck and grabbed a high-beam flash-light from his glove box, then got out of the car and surveyed the area. It was impossible to tell if he was on the land Jim owned or not. But he would walk until morning, until every square inch of property that he could cover had been checked.

He turned on the flashlight and then cried out her name. He listened intently, but there was no response. *That doesn't mean anything,* he told himself, fighting a wave of hopelessness. She might not be close enough to hear him. She might not be here at all.

Still, he couldn't let go of the last of his hope. If she wasn't someplace out here, then he was afraid they'd never find her.

He began to walk in a grid-like fashion, flashing his light left and right and stopping occasionally to call her name. Night had swooped down, making it impossible for him to see beyond the glow of his flashlight.

With each minute that ticked by, with every step he took, the fragile grasp on hope that he had loosened a little. Tears blurred his eyes, making it difficult for him to see.

He'd already lost so much in his life. He'd lost his parents when he was too young, his sister, Cherry, and his brother Sam. Wasn't that enough?

He paused as he thought he heard a sound in the distance. It was too late for anyone to mow their lawn and in any case he was too far away from any houses to hear a lawn mower.

Cocking his head, he tried to discern the direction of the sound. It seemed to be coming from someplace to his left. As he continued to look in that direction, he saw lights coming toward him. A tractor? Who would possibly be riding a tractor at this time of night?

He stood frozen, his flashlight beam pointed at the lights as the noise grew louder as the tractor came closer. *Definitely a tractor,* he thought.

As his beam found the rider, a painful gasp escaped him. He ran toward the moving machine.

Melanie clung to the steering wheel, her face wraith-like in the beam of his flashlight. As he reached the tractor, she shut off the engine, and in the immediate silence she released a deep sob. "I can't walk," she cried.

"I know." His heart beat so fast, so furious, he could scarcely talk. She was alive.

"No, I really can't walk. I think he broke my other ankle."

As Adam shone the beam of his flashlight on her swollen left ankle, on the bloody knees that showed through her torn pants, on her elbows, which were also raw and bleeding, rage momentarily stole his vision.

"He thought I was a helpless cripple, but I showed him." The words came from her in a sound that was half hysterical laughter and another deep sob.

"Come on. Let's get you out of here." Adam reached up for her and she collapsed into his arms and buried her face in the hollow of his throat and began to sob in earnest.

He asked no questions as he carried her to his truck. It was enough that she was safe in his arms. It wasn't until he had her in his passenger seat that she told him what had happened, how Jim had drugged her and taken her from the alley, how he had some kind of strange obsession that they were deeply in love before she left for New York and how he believed she'd abandoned him.

When she told him about Jim stomping on her good foot, he wanted to kill the man. He didn't call Cameron until they reached the hospital, where she was immediately whisked away from him and into the emergency room.

As Adam stood in the waiting room, he took out his phone and punched in Cameron's number. The sheriff answered on the first ring. "I've got her," Adam said.

"Where are you?"

Adam had already decided what he intended to tell Cameron, a slight misrepresentation of the truth in order to assure that Jim Collins would be where Adam wanted him to be.

"We're here at the hospital. She's unconscious, so I don't know what happened."

"Where did you find her?"

"Near the café. She was on the side of the road. It was just a matter of chance that I saw her at all. She's in bad shape, Cameron."

"We'll be right there."

Adam slipped his phone back into his pocket and once again fought against a rage that knew no boundaries. He'd love to see the look on Jim Collins's face when he heard the news that she'd been found by the Cowboy Café. The fact that Jim would be told that she was unconscious and had been unable to talk to Adam and was in bad shape would make the deputy believe that he still might be safe.

No place on earth was Deputy Jim Collins a safe man tonight. He couldn't find a hole deep enough, a tree high enough that Adam wouldn't be there waiting for him.

The agony that Melanie must have endured over the past hours pierced his very soul. She had to have suffered not only incredible physical pain but also mental anguish.

Pride surged up inside him as he thought about her slow, painful trek to the tractor. She was the strongest woman he'd ever met, and no matter how the two of them ended up, he would always be proud that he had known her, that he had loved her.

It didn't take long for Cameron and several of the other deputies to arrive. As they all came through the emergency room door, Adam was pleased to see Jim among the group.

"How is she?" Cameron asked worriedly as the rest of the men crowded around Adam.

It didn't take much for Adam to will tears to his eyes. "The doctor doesn't know if she's going to make it or not. She was beaten so badly." Adam gazed at Jim as he spoke the last words, and didn't miss the confusion that darkened the man's eyes.

Adam choked back a sob. "No matter what happens, I know she'd want me to thank all of you for your efforts." He shook Cameron's hand and then moved to Ben Temple and shook his, as well. When he reached

Jim, he clapped him on the back, then stepped back and sucker punched him in the nose.

Adam felt the satisfying crunch of cartilage as Jim yelped, fell backward to the floor and raised a hand to his blood-pumping nose.

"Hey!" Cameron yelled and stepped between the two.

"She wasn't unconscious," Adam said quickly. "She told me everything." He looked at Jim's bloody face as the man scrambled to his feet. "She told me how you took her out of that alley and drove her to your land, then stomped on her ankle to assure that she couldn't move. But she did move, you bastard. She managed to crawl to your tractor."

Jim took a step backward, his gaze darting to the outside door, but Ben grabbed his arm so any escape would be difficult.

"Jim, what in the hell have you done?" Cameron asked as he pulled his cuffs from his belt.

Adam thought Jim intended to deny it all, but suddenly his features crumpled into themselves as he looked around at the men who were his coworkers. "She was my soul mate. We were supposed to build a life together but she left me to go dance in New York. She had to pay for that. Don't you see? She left me broken and she had to pay."

Cameron cuffed him and then handed him over to Ben. "Get him the hell out of here," he said with disgust. "Lock him up and we'll see if the next soul mate he finds is a prison cell mate."

As Ben led Jim away, Cameron turned back to Adam. "So how is she really?"

"She went directly into surgery. He did a number on her ankle and broke it. Other than that, she's remarkably fine. She's beautiful and strong.... She's amazing."

"You probably saved her life by thinking of Jim," Cameron said.

"No." Adam shook his head firmly. "She saved her own life." Once again pride buoyed up inside him. Melanie didn't need him; she would do fine on her own. He just wished she wanted him in her life as much as he wanted her.

He and Cameron sat in chairs as Melanie was in surgery. Adam told the sheriff everything Melanie had related to him on the drive to the hospital.

"According to Melanie their relationship was all in his mind. They'd dated a couple of times, casual dates, but he fantasized an entire future with her and was enraged when she wasn't a part of it," Adam explained.

Cameron shook his head. "He was right under my nose. Why didn't I see it? Why didn't I even think about it? He was sick with his rage and I don't know why I didn't even see a hint of it."

"Those were the same kinds of questions I asked myself when Sam was arrested," Adam replied. "I thought I'd missed so many clues, but Sam hid his rage well, just like Jim did." He tried to stay focused on the conversation, but his thoughts were on Melanie.

Hopefully the surgeon would be able to fix whatever damage she'd sustained. He knew she'd depended on her one good foot to maneuver as well as she did around her house.

"Looks like I'm going to be hunting for a new deputy," Cameron said, pulling Adam's attention back to the conversation. "When this investigation is all over and done, come talk to me and we'll see what happens."

"Thanks," Adam replied. "I'll do that."

Minutes later he was alone in the waiting room. Cameron had headed back to the sheriff's office to interrogate Jim and all the other deputies had left, as well, to collect whatever they could to build a solid case against one of their own.

It was an hour later when Dr. Rice, the surgeon, came out to greet him. Adam jumped to his feet, instantly assured by the smile on the older man's face.

"We've patched her up. She took a couple of stitches on both knees and the ankle had to be reset and she's now sporting a couple of pins to help the ankle bone grow back properly, but she'll be fine. She's a tough one."

"Can I see her?" Adam asked, needing to check for himself that she was truly okay.

"We've just moved her to room fifteen. She's still pretty groggy, but you can go on in."

Adam didn't wait to hear anything else. He half ran down the hallway to room fifteen, which was semidark with just a small light glowing upward over the bed.

Her eyes were closed and she looked tiny and fragile, but he knew that was a false appearance. He knew the strength of will she had inside her and it awed him.

He slipped into the chair next to her bed and fought

the impulse to lean forward and take one of her slender, graceful hands in his. It wasn't his place to hold her hand. He was simply her boarder—the cowboy renting rooms upstairs—and that was it.

Chapter 18

Melanie awoke to the quiet of the hospital around her and she knew it must be the middle of the night. Her first realization was that she must still be drugged, because she felt no real pain anywhere in her body. Her second realization was that Adam was slumped down in a chair next to her bed, a faint snoring coming from him.

Her heart swelled with emotion. How had he managed to find her? He'd appeared like a knight in shining armor in the darkness of the night.

She closed her eyes and thought of that single moment when she'd finally reached the tractor seat, twisted the key, and nothing had happened. She had cried tears of fear, of frustration and exhaustion, and then she'd realized she needed to push in the clutch for the engine to start.

The foot that needed to push the clutch in was the one that Jim had stomped on. She managed to get her foot on the clutch and knew she'd probably only have one shot at pressing down before the pain would prove too much.

She'd screamed as she pressed in the clutch and turned the key. When the engine turned over, she used the hand throttle to keep it running as she fought to keep herself from fainting.

The tractor had been in first gear, moving at a snail's pace, but she knew there was no way she could press the clutch in again to change gears.

And then Adam had appeared. Her heart, her soul, he'd been there to save her. She opened her eyes once again and found herself staring into the blue depths of his.

"Hi," he said. "How are you feeling?" He leaned forward, as if needing to get closer to her.

"A little woozy. Was my ankle broken?"

He nodded. "You're now sporting some metal in that ankle and a brand-new cast. You also have a couple of stitches in your knees."

"And Jim?"

"Is in jail." He offered her one of his slow, sexy smiles. "Unfortunately he had an accident with my fist and suffered a broken nose just before he was arrested."

"Thank you," she said simply.

"Not a problem. I only wish I could have done more."

Tears suddenly burned in her eyes. "I don't know

what I would have done if you hadn't shown up when you did."

He leaned forward even more and took her hand in his. "You would have driven that tractor down Main Street directly to the sheriff's office. You would have been fine if I hadn't shown up." Admiration shone in his eyes. "I told you, Melanie, there's nothing you can't do except walk."

Her tears came faster. "I can't love you," she blurted out.

He squeezed her hand, a dark sadness gathering in his eyes. "I know you don't love me, Melanie."

"But I do love you and I can't."

He gazed at her, obviously confused. "Melanie, what are you saying?"

For the first time since she'd awakened, she felt the pain in her ankle, the familiar pain in her leg, but none of it compared to the pain that stabbed at her heart.

"Oh Adam, I'm probably going to be in a wheelchair for the rest of my life."

"And your point is?" he asked.

She swallowed hard against her tears, knowing she had to stay strong. "I would never want to burden you with me. You deserve so much more than I can be in your life." With each word her heart broke a little more. "I can't give you children and then chase after them when they learn to walk."

"There's nothing wrong with hiring a nanny for extra help," he replied calmly.

He always made things sound so easy, she thought.

He never saw the obstacles that she did. And yet every obstacle she had seen in the path that they had shared together had magically disappeared with him at her side.

His eyes shone with a light that threatened to steal her breath away. "Melanie, I love you and I have a feeling that rather than you being a burden on me, I'd spend most of my time chasing after you as you went about the business of living. Give us a chance, Melanie. If you love me half as much as I do you, then I know we can make it work."

She tried to think of all the reasons why it wouldn't work, but at the same time she realized one of the gifts he'd given her was the knowledge that she could do whatever she set her mind to. She'd done it tonight. Even though she couldn't walk, she'd managed to escape a man who wanted her dead.

A ray of hope began to shine in her heart, hope that maybe she could be enough for him, that she deserved him. "When you look at me that way, you make me believe that all things are possible," she said softly.

He stroked his hand tenderly down the side of her face. "Haven't you heard the old saying that with love all things are possible?"

"Kiss me, Adam, and make me truly believe."

He stood and leaned over her and placed his lips over hers. The kiss began soft and tender and grew in intensity until it held all the desire, all the love he felt for her. And with the emotions she tasted in his kiss, she believed in him, in their love, but most importantly, she believed in herself.

She could be what he wanted, what he needed. Despite her limitations he loved her and he believed in her. As the kiss ended, he leaned back and eyed her worriedly.

"You aren't so doped up from your operation that you won't remember any of this tomorrow, are you?"

She smiled. "I don't think so, but if I am, I'm sure you'll remind me. And now I have a question to ask you."

"What's that?"

Her smile deepened as joy filled her heart, the kind of joy she once felt while dancing. "How fast can you move your things from upstairs to my room?"

"Consider it already done," he replied and then took her lips in another kiss, which washed away any doubts that might have lingered in her head.

She could see their future, as bright as stage lights, as full of joy as dancing. It was filled with laughter and the kind of love that would last a lifetime.

It was almost dawn when Sheriff Cameron Evans left the jail, disgusted by his newest prisoner, exhausted from the long hours and yearning for a couple hours of sleep before he'd have to be at work once again.

He'd grilled Jim for a long time in an attempt to find out if he'd killed the waitresses as well as tried to kill Melanie Brooks, but while Jim had confessed everything he'd done to Melanie, he'd adamantly denied having anything to do with the two murders.

Unfortunately Cameron believed him, and that meant there was still a killer walking the streets of Grady Gulch. Cameron had a sick feeling in his stomach that it wasn't just a matter of *if* the killer would strike again. It was only a matter of *when*.

* * * * *

COMING NEXT MONTH FROM
HARLEQUIN® ROMANTIC SUSPENSE

Available January 22, 2013

#1739 BEYOND VALOR • *Black Jaguar Squadron*
by Lindsay McKenna

Though these two soldiers face death day after day, their greatest risk is taking a chance on each other.

#1740 A RANCHER'S DANGEROUS AFFAIR
Vengeance in Texas • by Jennifer Morey

Eliza's husband has been murdered, and she's in love with his brother. As guilt and love go to battle, Brandon may be the only one who can save her.

#1741 SOLDIER UNDER SIEGE • *The Hunted*
by Elle Kennedy

Special Forces soldier Tate doesn't trust anyone...especially the gorgeous woman who shows up on his doorstep asking him to kill a man.

#1742 THE LIEUTENANT BY HER SIDE
by Jean Thomas

Clare Fuller is forced to steal a mysterious amulet from army ranger Mark Griggs, but falling in love with him isn't in the plan. Nor is the danger that stalks them.

HRSCNM0113

REQUEST YOUR FREE BOOKS!
2 FREE NOVELS PLUS 2 FREE GIFTS!

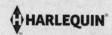

ROMANTIC suspense

Sparked by danger, fueled by passion

YES! Please send me 2 FREE Harlequin® Romantic Suspense novels and my 2 FREE gifts (gifts are worth about $10). After receiving them, if I don't wish to receive any more books, I can return the shipping statement marked "cancel." If I don't cancel, I will receive 4 brand-new novels every month and be billed just $4.49 per book in the U.S. or $5.24 per book in Canada. That's a savings of at least 14% off the cover price! It's quite a bargain! Shipping and handling is just 50¢ per book in the U.S. and 75¢ per book in Canada.* I understand that accepting the 2 free books and gifts places me under no obligation to buy anything. I can always return a shipment and cancel at any time. Even if I never buy another book, the two free books and gifts are mine to keep forever.

240/340 HDN FVS7

Name	(PLEASE PRINT)	
Address		Apt. #
City	State/Prov.	Zip/Postal Code
Signature (if under 18, a parent or guardian must sign)		

Mail to the Harlequin® Reader Service:
IN U.S.A.: P.O. Box 1867, Buffalo, NY 14240-1867
IN CANADA: P.O. Box 609, Fort Erie, Ontario L2A 5X3

**Want to try two free books from another line?
Call 1-800-873-8635 or visit www.ReaderService.com.**

* Terms and prices subject to change without notice. Prices do not include applicable taxes. Sales tax applicable in N.Y. Canadian residents will be charged applicable taxes. Offer not valid in Quebec. This offer is limited to one order per household. Not valid for current subscribers to Harlequin Romantic Suspense books. All orders subject to credit approval. Credit or debit balances in a customer's account(s) may be offset by any other outstanding balance owed by or to the customer. Please allow 4 to 6 weeks for delivery. Offer available while quantities last.

Your Privacy—The Harlequin® Reader Service is committed to protecting your privacy. Our Privacy Policy is available online at www.ReaderService.com or upon request from the Harlequin Reader Service.

We make a portion of our mailing list available to reputable third parties that offer products we believe may interest you. If you prefer that we not exchange your name with third parties, or if you wish to clarify or modify your communication preferences, please visit us at www.ReaderService.com/consumerchoice or write to us at Harlequin Reader Service Preference Service, P.O. Box 9062, Buffalo, NY 14269. Include your complete name and address.

HRS13

"How *did* you find me, Eva? I'm not exactly listed in any phone books."

She rested her suddenly shaky hands on her knees. "Someone told me you might be able to help me, so I decided to track you down. I'm…well, let's just say I'm very skilled when it comes to computers."

His jaw tensed.

"You're good, too," she added with grudging appreciation. "You left so many false trails it made me dizzy. But you slipped up in Costa Rica, and it led me here."

Tate let out a soft whistle. "I'm impressed. Very impressed, actually." He made a tsking sound. "You went to a lot of trouble to find me. Maybe it's time you tell me why."

"I told you—I need your help."

He raised one large hand and rubbed the razor-sharp stubble coating his strong chin.

A tiny thrill shot through her as she watched the oddly seductive gesture and imagined how it would feel to have those calloused fingers stroking her own skin, but that thrill promptly fizzled when she realized her thoughts had drifted off course again. What was it about this man that made her so darn aware of his masculinity?

She shook her head, hoping to clear her foggy brain, and met Tate's expectant expression. "Your help," she repeated.

"Oh really?" he drawled. "My help to do what?"

God, could she do this? How did one even begin to approach something like—

"For Chrissake, sweetheart, spit it out. I don't have all night."

She swallowed. Twice.

He started to push back his chair. "Screw it. I don't have time for—"

"I want you to kill Hector Cruz," she blurted out.

**Will Eva's secret be the ultimate unraveling of their fragile trust? Or will an overwhelming desire do them both in? Find out what happens next in
SOLDIER UNDER SIEGE**

Available February 2013 only from Harlequin Romantic Suspense wherever books are sold.

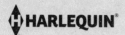

NOCTURNE

They never expected to fall for each other…

She's a committed sergeant in a top secret military unit.
He's a reluctant recruit—and a shape-shifter. But sparks fly
when Kristine and Quinn masquerade as honeymooners on a
beautiful island in search of Quinn's missing brother and his
new bride. Can the unlikely pair set aside their differences
in order to catch a killer bent on destroying Alpha Force?

FIND OUT IN

UNDERCOVER WOLF,

a sexy, adrenaline-fueled new tale in the
Alpha Force miniseries from

LINDA O. JOHNSTON

**Available February 5, 2013,
from Harlequin® Nocturne™.**

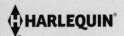
HARLEQUIN®

NOCTURNE

Discover

THE KEEPERS: L.A.,

a dark and epic new paranormal quartet
led by *New York Times* bestselling author

HEATHER GRAHAM

New Keeper Rhiannon Gryffald has her peacekeeping
duties cut out for her. Because in Hollywood, it's hard
to tell the actors from the werewolves, bloodsuckers and
shape-shifters. When Rhiannon hears about a string of
murders that bear all the hallmarks of a vampire serial
killer, she must unite forces with sexy undercover
Elven agent Brodie to uncover a plot that may forever
alter the face of human-paranormal relations....

KEEPER OF THE NIGHT

by **Heather Graham,**
coming **December 18, 2012.**
And look for

Keeper of the Moon by Harley Jane Kozack—
Available March 5, 2013
Keeper of the Shadows by Alexandra Sokoloff—
Available May 7, 2013
Keeper of the Dawn by Heather Graham—
Available July 1, 2013

HARLEQUIN®

NOCTURNE

Secrets, Suspense and Seduction…

Deep in the woods, wolf-shifter Nick Jenner is compelled
to help beautiful Mia D'Alessandro after she's bitten by a
feral wolf—a bite that could destroy her unless she bonds
with a pack in time. But Mia's not all she seems….

In a race against time, can they learn to trust each other
and their fragile new bond in order to overcome the evil
that threatens to destroy everything they hold dear?

FIND OUT IN

THE WOLF'S SURRENDER

by

KENDRA LEIGH CASTLE

**Available March 5, 2013,
from Harlequin® Nocturne™.**

www.Harlequin.com

HN88566